T0109972

Vladimir Nabokov

Lolita:

A SCREENPLAY

Vladimir Nabokov was born in St. Petersburg on April 23, 1899. His family fled to the Crimea in 1917, during the Bolshevik Revolution, then went into exile in Europe. Nabokov studied at Trinity College, Cambridge, earning a degree in French and Russian literature in 1922, and lived in Berlin and Paris for the next two decades, writing prolifically, mainly in Russian, under the pseudonym Sirin. In 1940 he moved to the United States, where he pursued a brilliant literary career (as a poet, novelist, memoirist, critic, and translator) while teaching Russian, creative writing, and literature at Stanford, Wellesley, Cornell, and Harvard. The monumental success of his novel *Lolita* (1955) enabled him to give up teaching and devote himself fully to his writing. In 1961 he moved to Montreux, Switzerland, where he died in 1977. Recognized as one of the master prose stylists of the century in both Russian and English, he translated a number of his original English works—including *Lolita*—into Russian, and collaborated on English translations of his original Russian works.

INTERNATIONAL

BOOKS BY *Vladimir Nabokov*

Lolita:

A SCREENPLAY

Lolita:

A SCREENPLAY

BY *Vladimir Nabokov*

VINTAGE INTERNATIONAL

VINTAGE BOOKS

A DIVISION OF RANDOM HOUSE, INC.

NEW YORK

FIRST VINTAGE INTERNATIONAL EDITION, JUNE 1997

Library of Congress Cataloging-in-Publication Data
Nabokov, Vladimir Vladimirovich, 1899–1977.
Lolita : a screenplay / by Vladimir Nabokov. — 1st Vintage International
ed.
p. cm.
Originally published : New York : McGraw-Hill, 1974.
ISBN: 978-0-679-77255-2
I. Lolita (Motion picture) II. Title.
PN1997.L66   1997
791.43'72—dc20   96-30305
CIP

Random House Web address: http://www.randomhouse.com/

To Véra

This is the purely Nabokov version of the screenplay and not the same version which was produced as the motion picture *Lolita,* distributed by Metro-Goldwyn-Mayer, Inc.

Lolita:

A SCREENPLAY

Foreword

Sometime at the end of July 1959 (my pocket diary does not
give the exact date), in Arizona, where my wife and I were
hunting butterflies, with headquarters at Forest Houses (between Flagstaff and Sedona), I received through Irving Lazar
who was representing me a message from Messrs. Harris &
Kubrick. They had acquired the film rights of *Lolita* in 1958,
and were now asking me to come over to Hollywood and
write the script. The honorarium they offered was considerable, but the idea of tampering with my own novel caused
me only revulsion. A certain lull in the activity of the local
lepidoptera suggested, however, that we might just as well
drive on to the West Coast. After a meeting in Beverly Hills
(at which I was told that in order to appease the censor a
later scene should contain some pudic hint to the effect that
Humbert had been secretly married to Lolita all along),
followed by a week of sterile meditation on the shores of Lake
Tahoe (where a calamitous growth of manzanita precluded
the presence of good butterflies), I decided not to undertake
the job and left for Europe.

We sojourned in Paris, London, Rome, Taormina, Genoa,
and Lugano, where we arrived for a week's stay on December
9 (Grand Hotel, rooms 317–318, says my 1959 agenda,
which now grows more talkative). I had long ceased to bother
about the film, when suddenly I experienced a small nocturnal

illumination, of diabolical origin, perhaps, but unusually compelling in sheer bright force, and clearly perceived an attractive line of approach to a screen version of *Lolita*. I regretted having had to decline the offer and was aimlessly revolving bits of dream dialogue in my mind when magically a telegram came from Hollywood urging me to revise my earlier decision and promising me a freer hand.

We spent the rest of the winter in Milan, San-Remo, and Mentone and on Thursday, February 18, 1960, left for Paris (2 singles Mentone-Paris, beds 6 and 8, car 9, leaving 7:15 P.M., arriving 8:55 A.M., these and other informative items from my diary are mentioned not only for mnemonic comfort but because I have not the heart to leave them ignored and unused). The first lap of the long journey to Los Angeles began with a rather ominous gag: the damned sleeping car stopped before reaching the platform, amid the mimosas and cypresses in the aquarelle elegance of a Riviera evening, and my wife and I, and the almost demented porter, had to swarm up from ground level to board the train.

By next evening we were at Le Havre, on the *United States*. We had booked an upper-deck cabin (61) but were transferred at no extra cost, with a bonus of fruit and whiskey, to a charming suite (65) by courtesy of the charming management—one of the many treats an American writer is granted. On Saturday, February 27, after four busy days in New York, we left for Chicago (10 P.M., car 551, bedrooms en suite E–F, enjoyable jottings, naive trivia of yore!) and next evening boarded the Super Chief on which the next installment of our bedrooms welcomed us with a twin burst of music, whereupon we scrambled frantically to stop, kill, stamp out, annihilate the heinous gadget and, not finding the switch, had to call for help (of course, the situation is incomparably worse on Soviet trains where you are strictly forbidden to turn off the muzakovitch).

On March 1, Kubrick and I, at his Universal City studio,

debated in an amiable battle of suggestion and countersuggestion how to cinemize the novel. He accepted all my vital points, I accepted some of his less significant ones. Next morning, sitting on a bench under a lovely bright yellow-green *Pyrospodia* tree in a public park not far from the Beverly Hills Hotel (one of whose cottages Mr. Lazar had taken for us) I was already attending with all my wits to the speech and pantomime in my head. On March 9, Kubrick had us meet Tuesday Weld (a graceful ingénue but not my idea of Lolita). On March 10 we rented, from the late John Francis Fay, a pleasant villa (2088 Mandeville Canyon Road). On March 11, Kubrick sent me by messenger a rough outline of the scenes he and I had agreed upon: they covered Part One of the novel. By then his attitude had convinced me that he was willing to heed my whims more closely than those of the censor.

During the next months we met rather seldom—every fortnight or so, at his place or mine; outlines ceased altogether, criticism and advice got briefer and briefer, and by midsummer I did not feel quite sure whether Kubrick was serenely accepting whatever I did or silently rejecting everything.

I worked with zest, composing mentally every morning from eight to noon while butterfly hunting in the hot hills, which, except for some remarkably skittish individuals of a little-known Wood Nymph, produced nothing noteworthy, but *per contra* teemed with rattlers whose hysterical performance in the undergrowth or in the middle of the trail was more comical than alarming. After a leisurely lunch, prepared by the German cook who came with the house, I would spend another four-hour span in a lawn chair, among the roses and mockingbirds, using lined index cards and a Blackwing pencil, for copying and recopying, rubbing out and writing anew, the scenes I had imagined in the morning.

By nature I am no dramatist; I am not even a hack scenarist; but if I had given as much of myself to the stage or the screen as I have to the kind of writing which serves a triumphant life sentence between the covers of a book, I would have advocated and applied a system of total tyranny, directing the play or the picture myself, choosing settings and costumes, terrorizing the actors, mingling with them in the bit part of guest, or ghost, prompting them, and, in a word, pervading the entire show with the will and art of one individual—for there is nothing in the world that I loathe more than group activity, that communal bath where the hairy and slippery mix in a multiplication of mediocrity. All I could do in the present case was to grant words primacy over action, thus limiting as much as possible the intrusion of management and cast. I persevered in the task until I could tolerate the rhythm of the dialogue and properly control the flow of the film from motel to motel, mirage to mirage, nightmare to nightmare. Long before, in Lugano, I had adumbrated the sequence at the Enchanted Hunters Hotel, but its exact mechanism now proved tremendously difficult to adjust so as to render by the transparent interplay of sound effects and trick shots both a humdrum morning and a crucial moment in the lives of a desperate pervert and a wretched child. A small number of scenes (for example, McCoo's phantom house, the three poolside nymphs, or Diana Fowler starting to repeat the fatal cycle through which Charlotte Haze had passed) are based on unused material that I had kept after destroying the MS. of my novel, an act which I regret less than my having discarded those passages.

By the end of June, after having used up over a thousand cards, I had the thing typed, sent to Kubrick the four hundred pages it made, and, needing a rest, was driven by my wife in a rented Impala to Inyo County for a short stay at Glacier Lodge on Big Pine Creek, where we collected the Inyo Blue and other nice bugs in the surrounding mountains. Upon our returning to Mandeville Canyon, Kubrick visited us to say that my screenplay was much too unwieldly, contained too many unnecessary episodes, and would take about seven hours to run. He wanted several deletions and other changes, and some of these I did make, besides devising new sequences and situations, when preparing a shorter script which he got in September and said was fine. That last stretch was the toughest, but also the most exhilarating part of the six-month task. Ten years later, though, I reread my play and restored a few scenes.

My final meeting with Kubrick must have taken place on September 25, 1960, at his house in Beverly Hills: he showed me that day photographs of Sue Lyon, a demure nymphet of fourteen or so, who, said Kubrick, could be easily made to look younger and grubbier for the part of Lolita for which he already had signed her up. On the whole I felt rather pleased with the way things had worked out, when on October 12, at P.M., my wife and I took the Super Chief (bdr. E + F, car 181) for Chicago, changing there to the Twentieth-Century (bdr J–K, car 261) and reaching New York, at 8:30 A.M. on October 15. In the course of that splendid journey— and the following note can stir only the dedicated extra-sensorialist—I had a dream (October 13) in which I saw written: "They say on the radio that she is as natural as Sarah Footer." I have never known anybody of that name.

Complacency is a state of mind that exists only in retrospective: it has to be shattered before being ascertained. Mine was to endure for a year and a half. As early as October 28 (New York, Hampshire House, room 503) I find the following plan penciled in my little book: "a novel, a life, a love—which is only the elaborate commentary to a gradually evolved short poem." The "short poem" started to become a rather long one soon after the *Queen Elizabeth* ("Buy dental floss, new pince-nez, Bonamine, check with baggage-master big black trunk on pier before embarcation, Deck A, Cabin 71") deposited us at Cherbourg on November 7. Four days later, at the Principe e Savoia in Milan and then throughout the winter in Nice, in a rented flat (57 Promenade des Anglais) and after that in Tessin, Valais, and Vaud ("Oct. 1, 1961, moved to Montreux-Palace") I was absorbed in *Pale Fire,* which I finished on December 4, 1961. Lepidopterology, work on the galleys of my *Eugene Onegin* mammoth, and the revising of a difficult translation (*The Gift*) took care of the spring of 1962, spent mostly in Montreux, so that (apart from the fact that nobody insisted on my coming to Elstree) the shooting of the *Lolita* film in England was begun and concluded far beyond the veil of my vanities.

On May 31, 1962 (almost exactly twenty-two years after we emigrated from St.-Nazaire aboard the *Champlain*), the *Queen Elizabeth* took us to New York for the opening of *Lolita.* Our cabin (main deck, cabin 95) was quite as comfortable as the one we had on the *Champlain* in 1940 and, moreover, at a cocktail party given by the purser (or surgeon, my scribble is illegible), he turned to me and said: Now you, as an American businessman, will enjoy the following story (story not recorded). On June 6 I revisited my old haunts, the entomological department at the American Museum of Natural History, where I deposited the specimens of Chapman's Hairstreak I had taken the previous April between Nice and Grasse, under strawberry trees. The première took place on June 13 (Loew's State, BW at 45, E2 + 4 orchestra, "horrible seats" says my outspoken agenda). Crowds were awaiting the limousines that drew up one by one, and there I, too, rode, as eager and innocent as the fans who peered into my car hoping to glimpse James Mason but finding only the placid profile of a stand-in for Hitchcock. A few days before, at a private screening, I had discovered that Kubrick was a great director, that his *Lolita* was a first-rate film with magnificent actors, and that only ragged odds and ends of my script had been used. The modifications, the garbling of my best little finds, the omission of entire scenes, the addition of new ones, and all sorts of other changes may not have been sufficient to erase my name from the credit titles but they certainly made the picture as unfaithful to the original script as an American poet's translation from Rimbaud or Pasternak.

I hasten to add that my present comments should definitely not be construed as reflecting any belated grudge, any high-pitched deprecation of Kubrick's creative approach. When adapting *Lolita* to the speaking screen he saw my novel in one way, I saw it in another—that's all, nor can one deny that infinite fidelity may be an author's ideal but can prove a producer's ruin.

My first reaction to the picture was a mixture of aggravation, regret, and reluctant pleasure. Quite a few of the extraneous inventions (such as the macabre ping-pong scene or that rapturous swig of Scotch in the bathtub) struck me as appropriate and delightful. Others (such as the collapsing cot or the frills of Miss Lyon's elaborate nightgown) were painful. Most of the sequences were not really better than those I had so carefully composed for Kubrick, and I keenly regretted the waste of my time while admiring Kubrick's fortitude in enduring for six months the evolution and infliction of a useless product.

But I was wrong. Aggravation and regret soon subsided as I recollected the inspiration in the hills, the lawn chair under the jacaranda, the inner drive, the glow, without which my task could not have been accomplished. I told myself that nothing had been wasted after all, that my scenario remained intact in its folder, and that one day I might publish it—not in pettish refutation of a munificent film but purely as a vivacious variant of an old novel.

Vladimir Nabokov
Montreux
December, 1973

Prologue

SOUND TRACK:

A feminine voice (Lolita's, or rather Dolly Schiller's) repeats exactly a fragment of speech from her last conversation with Humbert at the end of Act Three:

. . . Oh, what does it matter. Up in Parkington, I guess. He's got a house there, a regular old castle (*rustle of rummaging*). There was a picture of it somewhere. (*flip-flip*) Yes, here it is.

Pavor Manor, an Elaborate, Antiquated Wooden Mansion at the Top of a Winding Forest Road

This is Clare Quilty's lair, not far from Parkington, Ramsdale County. The sun is rising above the gnarled old trees. After a brief still, the CAMERA glides around an ornate turret and dips into an upper-story casement. A prone sleeper (Quilty) is glimpsed in dorsal view. The CAMERA also locates the drug addict's implementa on a bedside chair, and with a shudder withdraws. It slides down the gutter pipe, returns to the porch and meets a car which stops in the driveway. Humbert Humbert, hatless, raincoated, emerges. Lurching a little (he is drunk), he makes for the front door. He rings the doorbell. He uses the knocker. There is no response. He rings and knocks again. Still no response. With a petulant snarl, he pushes the door—and it swings open as in a medieval fairy tale.

CUT TO:

A Spacious and Ugly Hall with a Long Mirror and a Huge Boar's Head on the Wall
Humbert enters. With a drunkard's fussy care he closes the door behind him. He looks around. He produces a pistol.

CUT TO:

The Central Staircase
down which slowly comes a large man (Clare Quilty) in a silk dressing gown, the sash of which he is tying as he goes. The host sees the visitor. They face each other. Now begins a silent shadowy sequence which should not last more than one minute. As Humbert levels his weapon, Quilty retreats and majestically walks upstairs. Humbert fires. Once more. We see him missing: the impact of a bullet sets a rocking chair performing on the landing. Then he hits a picture (photograph of Duk-Duk ranch which Lolita had visited). Next a large ugly vase is starred and smashed. Finally, on his fourth fire, he stops a grandfather clock in its clacking stride. The fifth bullet wounds Quilty, and the last one fells him on the upper landing.

CUT TO:

Dr. John Ray
a psychiatrist, perusing a manuscript on his desk. He swings around toward us in his swivel chair.

DR. RAY   I'm Dr. John Ray. Pleased to meet you. This here is a bundle of notes, a rough autobiography, poorly

[2]

typed, which Mr. Humbert Humbert wrote after his arrest, in prison, where he was held without bail on a charge of murder, and in the psychopathic ward where he was committed for observation. Without this document his crime would have remained unexplained. Naturally, in my capacity of psychotherapist, I would have preferred obtaining the information revealed here not from the typewriter but from the couch.

The murder Humbert perpetrated is only a side product of his case. His memoir is mainly an account of his fatal infatuation with a certain type of very young girl and of the torments he underwent in his vortex of libido and guilt. I have no intention to glorify Humbert. He is horrible, he is abject. He is a shining example of moral leprosy. But there are in his story depths of passion and suffering, patterns of tenderness and distress, that cannot be dismissed by his judges. As a case history, his autobiography will no doubt become a classic in psychiatric circles. But more important to us is the ethical impact it should have on a serious audience. For here lurks a general lesson: the wayward child, the egotistic mother, the panting maniac—these are not only vivid characters in a unique story. They warn us of dangerous trends. They point out potent evils. They should make all of us —parents, social workers, educators—apply ourselves with still greater vigilance and vision to the task of bringing up a better generation in a safer world. Thank you.

CUT TO:

Humbert's Cell in The Tombs
He is writing at a table. Conspicuous among the reference books at his elbow are some tattered travel guides and maps. Presently his voice surfaces as he rereads the first sentences of his story.

HUMBERT'S VOICE   I was born in Paris forty dark
years ago. My father was a gentle easy-going person, a
Swiss citizen of mixed French and Austrian descent with
a dash of the blue Danube in his veins. He owned a
luxurious hotel on the Riviera. In a minute I am going
to pass around some lovely picture postcards. My mother
was an Englishwoman. Her death preceded that of my
father by two decades: she was killed by a bolt of lightning during a picnic on my fourth birthday, high in the
Maritime Alps.

CUT TO:

*A Mountain Meadow—A thunderhead advancing above
sharp cliffs*
Several people scramble for shelter, and the first big drops of
rain strike the zinc of a lunchbox. As the poor lady in white
runs toward the pavilion of a lookout, a blast of livid light
fells her. Her graceful specter floats up above the black cliffs
holding a parasol and blowing kisses to her husband and child
who stand below, looking up, hand in hand.

CUT TO:

HUMBERT'S VOICE   Aunt Sybil, my mother's eldest
sister, a severe spinster, helped my father to bring me
up. My childhood was spent in the bright world of the
Hotel Mirana, at St.-Topaz.

CUT TO:

*A Picture Postcard of the Mirana Palace flying its flag in a
cloudless sky*
There are palm trees in front of it, and a system of stone steps

winding down from terrace to terrace, among rhododendrons and roses. Back to the memoirist's murmur:

HUMBERT'S VOICE   I remember a certain summer. My father was away in Naples attending to the affairs of an Italian lady he was courting at the time. In the east wing of our hotel an English family occupied a first-floor suite.

CUT TO:

Picture Postcard of Hotel
A clumsy cross is scrawled over one window.

HUMBERT'S VOICE   This was Annabel's room. How strange to recollect today, in the light of another love, those past pangs! I was fourteen and she was twelve, in that kingdom by the sea. Young as we were, we fell in love. My Aunt Sybil and Annabel's parents apparently realized that if she and I filched somehow five mad minutes of privacy, God knows what would come of it. Therefore, they saw to our not obtaining that privacy. In fact, *any* meeting between us was allowed only on condition we kept in the public domain. Good Lord, how I envy today's youngsters and their progressive Freudian freedom. Poor Humbert, poor Annabel. I would now like a shot of two hands.

CUT TO:

Two Young Hands—right boy's, left girl's—both slender, long-fingered, tanned, hers with the modest star of a topaz ring, his with fine glistening hair on the back of the wrist, and a wrist watch (11:55), creeping toward each other—belonging to Humbert and Annabel (who are prone on the beach, sunning their backs in symmetrical similar adjacent positions), now through shifting sifted sand, now under sand, now in the shimmer of midday—and now they meet like two wary sensitive insects—and suddenly separate, a pretty scene for the subtle camera as the shore-fortress gun booms noon.

CUT TO:

HUMBERT'S VOICE   I loved her more tenderly than Tristan adored Isolde, more hotly than Petrarca desired his Laura, more romantically than Poe loved little Virginia. Once, on a rosy rock in the purple sea, I made her promise me an old-fashioned assignation at night in the palmy hotel garden.

CUT TO:

Rocky Promontory
Annabel supine, Humbert murmuring passionate plaints. Two Englishmen, robust freckled swimmers, interrupt these throbbings.

CUT TO:

The Garden of the Mirana Palace at Night
On a lower lighted balcony Annabel's parents, Humbert's Aunt Sybil, and a Mr. Cooper are playing cards (poker, European fashion). Aunt Sybil narrowly fondles three kings. Annabel in pale pajamas slithers through the honeysuckle from a first-floor window into the dark garden where she is joined by young Humbert near the balustrade under the oleanders. She sits on a stone shelf, he worships her from below, his arms embracing her haunches, and the light of an ornamental lamp imprints on a stone wall the emblematic silhouettes of long leaves. He is groping his way to a secret fount

when her mother claps down her cards and loudly calls her daughter's name.

HUMBERT'S VOICE   And then summer was over. Aunt Sybil, after a torrential rain, broke her leg on a slippery terrace, and I was supposed that evening to sit at her bedside and read to her *South Wind*, her favorite novel; instead of which I escaped to the little railway station where the great European expresses so grandly stopped. I just made it—and saw Annabel off.

CUT TO:

A Côte d'Azur Station—luminous evening—black cypresses and a young moon
The *train bleu* is pulling out. We follow a youth trotting alongside the sleeping car *Nice-Paris* from the window of which the young girl he is seeing off leans out in an ecstasy of blown kisses and streaming tears.

HUMBERT'S VOICE   We parted. Never again did I see her alive. A few months after she left the Riviera I was sent to school in England. That same year she died of pneumonia in a seaside town. I learned of her illness at the last moment and barely managed to arrive in time for the funeral. This is her tomb at the end of that vista.

CUT TO:

That Vista
We see her highborn kinsmen, in a romantic Poe-esque arrangement, bearing her away down an alley of tall cypresses. Our young mourner watches, cloaked in his grief. A related nymphet places a wreath on the tomb.

HUMBERT'S VOICE   I am writing this in prison, and the physical seclusion I am condemned to here strangely helps to encompass and concentrate the remote, diffuse, personal past I'm evoking. If I am given enough time before my trial I hope to proceed onward from that first young love and relate in all possible detail of circumstance and emotion the story of my later life in Europe and America. And if I manage to finish my difficult task, I shall place these pages in the capable hands of my adviser and physician, Dr. John Ray.

CUT TO:

Dr. Ray in His Study as Before, holding the typescript

DR. RAY   And here they are, those precious pages. From them we learn that Humbert could never forget graceful Annabel, and her shape and shadow haunted him in every alley of his love life. He finished college in England and continued his graduate studies—in the field of comparative literature—in Switzerland, where his nationality and temperament kept him away from the tumult of World War Two. He then moved to Paris, where he engaged in various literary pursuits and taught English at a boys' school. But we are not concerned with his intellectual life. We are interested in his emotional tribulations. Everywhere: In public parks——

CUT TO:

A Nymphet Readjusts the Straps of Her Roller Skate
She has placed her armored foot on the edge of Humbert's bench, and her shining curls tumble over her sun-dappled bare leg.

DR. RAY'S VOICE   —at bus stops——

[8]

Chattering, Jostling Schoolgirls crowd into a bus and push against Humbert
One nymphet glances at him, nudges another lass, and both giggle.

DR. RAY'S VOICE   —on street corners——

CUT TO:

Two Nymphets play at marbles under a sidewalk maple

DR. RAY'S VOICE   —in the garden of an orphan-
        age——

CUT TO:

Pale, Black-stockinged Girls performing tame calisthenics directed by a nun

DR. RAY'S VOICE   —and in many other haunts, Hum-
        bert wrestled with strange wretched urges and kept
        searching for the child of his shameful obsession, for
        some incarnation of his boyhood sweetheart. At thirty,
        he decided to marry. His choice fell on the daughter of
        a Polish-born doctor in Paris who was treating him for
        a heart condition.

CUT TO:

Humbert and the Doctor—playing chess
The doctor's daughter Valeria flirts with Humbert. She is in her late twenties and rather shopworn and pudgy, but imitates in attitudes and attire a little girl "She looked fluffy and

frolicsome, dressed *à la gamine* . . . and pouted, and dimpled, and romped, and dirndled, in the cutest and tritest fashion imaginable."*

DR. RAY'S VOICE   He married Valeria, but reality soon asserted itself, and presently unsatisfied Humbert had on his hands not a nymphet but a large, puffy, dull, adult woman.

CUT TO:

A Bourgeois Evening in a Tiny Parisian Flat
Humbert reads the evening paper. Plump-shouldered, in a rumpled slip, scratching her rump, Valeria looks after the *pot-au-feu.*

DR. RAY'S VOICE   The marriage dragged on for several years. In the meantime, Humbert went on with his literary and educational studies. A handbook of French translations from English poetry enjoyed some success, and an Institute of Comparative Literature in an American city invited him to come over for a series of lectures.

CUT TO:

The Prefecture in Paris. Humbert and Valeria come out.
He is checking a batch of documents, she looks perturbed.

HUMBERT   We have all our papers now.

DR. RAY'S VOICE   They have all their papers now. They are all set to go. Good-bye, gray Paree!

* Passages in quotation marks denote excerpts from the novel *Lolita.*

HUMBERT   Good-bye, gray Paree. Now, my dear, don't lose your passport. (*Gives it to her.*)

They follow the sidewalk. A taxi starts creeping along the curb as if inviting them to take it. Valeria is silent, and keeps shaking her poodle head.

DR. RAY'S VOICE   Watch that cab.

HUMBERT   Why are you shaking your head? Something in it? A pebble?

She shakes it.

HUMBERT   I can assure you it is quite empty.

VALERIA   No-no-no-no-no——

HUMBERT   That will do.

VALERIA   ——I cannot go on with it. You will sail
alone.

HUMBERT   What? What's that, you fool?

VALERIA   We must separate.

HUMBERT   I refuse to discuss this in the street. Taxi!

The cab that had been quietly escorting them glides up.

HUMBERT   *Quarante-deux, rue Baudelaire.*

DR. RAY'S VOICE   Forty-two Baudelaire Street.

They get into the taxi.

HUMBERT   May I inquire *why* you want us to separate?

VALERIA   Because life with you is sad and horrible.
Because you've got impossible eyes. Because I cannot
imagine your thoughts. Because I'm afraid of you and
hate you.

DR. RAY'S VOICE   She had never been so voluble.

HUMBERT   You've never been so voluble before. All
right. Let's get this straight——

DR. RAY'S VOICE   My patient is flabbergasted. As
Professor Gast used to say: "Woe to him who gets
stuck in his own guilt complex like an angry fly." Mr.
Humbert cannot react rationally, he splutters. That's
the famous *Place de l'Etoile*, Place of the Star. Need
good brakes. Oops. See what I mean?

The taxi driver is strangely erratic.

VALERIA   It's all finished now. I'm going to be free.
There's another man in my life and I'm leaving you.

HUMBERT   What man? What are you talking about?
How dare you?

DR. RAY'S VOICE   Dare indeed. A very curious situa-
tion. Humbert is accustomed to making the decisions.
Now the fate of his marriage is no longer in his hands.
I think the cab driver ought to have turned left here.
Oh, well, he can take the next cross street.

[12]

VALERIA   He's a human being, not a monster. He's a White Russian. He was a colonel in the Russian army. His father was a Councilor of the Tsar.

HUMBERT   I don't know whom you are speaking of. I'll—I don't know what I'll do to you if you go on like that.

DR. RAY'S VOICE   Look out! Close shave. When you analyze those jaywalkers you find they hesitate between the womb and the tomb.

VALERIA   Oh, you can't do anything to me now— because I love him.

HUMBERT   But damn you—who the devil is he?

VALERIA   Him, of course (*points at the thick back-head of the driver who turns briefly revealing a Russian profile, potato nose, and bristly moustache.*)

The taxi pulls up at the curb.

CUT TO:

Sidewalk in Front of 42, rue Baudelaire.
The driver and both passengers get out of the cab.

DRIVER   I am Colonel Maximovich, allow me to present myself. I have seen you often in the cinema of the corner, and she was sitting between us. (*Smiles fondly at Valeria.*) Let us discuss.

HUMBERT   We have nothing to discuss.

MAXIMOVICH   Perhaps we can move her and her things immediately in my auto. (*turning to Valeria*) You want? You are prepared?

HUMBERT   I will not have anything to do with either of you. This is ridiculous.

MAXIMOVICH   She is quite pale today, the poor. You must permit me to help with her baggage.

VALERIA   The percolator!

MAXIMOVICH   Yes, all the presents of marriage. Also, the white dress, the black dress, library books which she must return, her furry coat, and her diet.

HUMBERT   I beg your pardon? What was that last fascinating item?

VALERIA   My diet. He means the printed list father gave me.

HUMBERT   Oh yes. Oh, of course. Anything else?

MAXIMOVICH   One will see. Let us mount upstairs.

DR. RAY'S VOICE   Divorce was inevitable. Valeria had found herself another, more suitable mate, and lone Humbert set out for America.

CUT TO:

Humbert Dramatically Standing on a Liner's Deck
The towers of New York loom in the autumnal mist.

DR. RAY'S VOICE For the following year Humbert had been promised a lectureship at Beardsley College in Idaho. Meanwhile in New York he spent all his time in libraries preparing his course, a series of lectures under the general title of "Romanticists and Rebels."

CUT TO:

Library
In the vicinity of Humbert's carrel a brood of bored school-girls are shown by their teacher The Place Where Books Live.

DR. RAY'S VOICE He also accepted lecture engagements out of town. A nervous breakdown in result of his solitary exertions and repressed dreams interrupted one such engagement at a Women's Club.

CUT TO:

A Women's Club
A full-blown matron, Mrs. Nancy Whitman (her name pinned to her breast), rises above a carafe to introduce the speaker.

MRS. WHITMAN Before introducing the distinguished visitor on tonight's program, you will be glad to learn that next Friday the well-known psychiatrist, Dr. John Ray, will talk to us on the sexual symbolism of golf.
(applause)
We have here tonight Dr. Humbert, who has spent many years in *very* continental surroundings, and who will talk to us right now on romantic poetry. Please, Dr. Humbert.

CUT TO:

Feminine Eyes Watching the Speaker—changing expressions come and go on various elastic faces
some plump, but changing to eights and snapping in a distorted mirror; others, lean and long, developing abysmal décolletés; others again blending with the flesh of rolling bare arms, or turning into wax fruit in arty bowls.

HUMBERT'S FALTERING VOICE   Let me illustrate my point by reading to you Edgar's poem about . . . about . . .

CUT TO:

The Lecturer is now shown clearly except for a ripple or two of optical interference

He fumbles feverishly through a volume to find a quotation he needs.

HUMBERT   I put a marker in, but it dropped out, evidently. Somebody ought to collect all the markers we shed. I'm sure, though, it was in this volume. Oh God, oh God . . .

He fumbles feverishly through a volume to find a quotation he needs.

HUMBERT   (*in a pearly sweat*) It is supposed to be a very complete anthology. There should be an index. Here it is, here it is. Oh, I must find that poem. It is sure to be here. It began with an "N": n, y, m. N, y, m. . . . n. y. m . . . Oh, I'm sure it began with an "N" as in "Annabel."

HELPFUL VOICE   Title or first line?

HUMBERT   Don't ask me. This is atrocious. The term I
wish to illustrate is "nymphet."

MURMURS IN AUDIENCE   What? What? What did
he say?

HUMBERT   After all, I don't really need this stupid
book. Stupid book, go!
          (*Tosses it away.*)
So the term is nymphet. I intend to introduce the following idea: Between the age limits of nine and fourteen
there are certain maidens: they bewitch the traveler who
is twice their age and reveal to him their true nature,
which is not human but nymphic—in other words,
demoniac—and these chosen creatures I propose to
designate as nymphets.

He is speaking very loud, almost screaming, and there is a
rising rumble in the audience.

HUMBERT   Let me finish, ladies. Now the question is:
between these age limits are *all* girl-children nymphets?
'Course, not. Otherwise the lone traveler would have long
gone insane. Neither are good looks any criterion. I am
speaking of a certain fey grace, of the elusive, shifty,
soul-shattering, insidious charm that separates the pre-
teen demon from the ordinary sweet round-faced child
with a tummy and pigtails. You have to be an artist
and a madman, a creature of infinite melancholy.——
Silence!

His audience is coming out of its stunned stupefaction.

HUMBERT   Yes, only a madman can really distinguish
at once—oh, at once—by ineffable signs—the feline out-

line of a cheekbone, the slenderness of a downy limb, and other indices which despair and shame and tears of tenderness forbid me to tab—tab—tabulate———

CUT TO:

Distorted Matronly Faces
and a good deal of rubbery, enveloping, adult flesh is now crowding Humbert out of the picture

HUMBERT   We cringe and hide, yes, but our dreams contain enchantments which normal men never know. What indeed could Edgar Poe see in Mother Clemm, the mother of his pubescent bride? Oh, how horrible full-grown women are to the nymphet-lover! Don't come near me! Hands off! I'm not well—I———

He faints.

CUT TO:

The Office of the Psychotherapeutic Home
Humbert, in a vicuña coat, applies for admission.

HUMBERT   I have come because I need help.

BUXOM RECEPTIONIST   And I'm sure you will get it. Have you filled that other form too? Okay.

HUMBERT   I want to say that I am perfectly aware of the real nature of my problems. All I need is some mental rest. Not a solution but solitude.

RECEPTIONIST   Dr. Ray will easily establish a working relationship with you.

HUMBERT   The point is I don't need a cure, because I'm incurable——

RECEPTIONIST   Oh, come. Everything and everybody can be cured. Sure.

HUMBERT   Well, anyway I'm not interested in being cured. What I need, what I badly need, is some kind of diversion, some peace of mind.

RECEPTIONIST   Our occupational therapy provides many fascinating contacts and outlets.

HUMBERT   I mean I have the feeling that something in my mind is poisoning everything else. I know this thing cannot be eliminated but perhaps it could be reduced to reasonable dimensions, watered down, so to speak.

RECEPTIONIST   Well, I'm sure Dr. Ray will fix all that. He'll assign you to a delightful group of patients we have here, mainly European immigrants. See these shoes?
            (*Proffers her foot.*)
A wonderful Hungarian patient made them for me. Aren't they something!

HUMBERT   Please tell Dr. Ray that I want a private room. And then I must have silence and peace all the time.

RECEPTIONIST   Oh, I must disagree with you there. I think silence is terrible. Let me try again. Dr. Ray's office.

[19]

DR. RAY'S VOICE   So it happened that in the nursing home where Humbert spent three weeks I met him and talked with him. The patient refused to reveal the reasons for his breakdown, but it was plain he needed relaxation. Tranquilizers and a regular mental regime brought considerable improvement to his condition. An acquaintance of his, whose cousin had an attractive house in Ramsdale on the beautiful lake of that name, suggested that Humbert come to lodge there during the summer, before traveling west to the university where he had been invited to teach.

Act One

Ramsdale, a pretty, sedate town with opulent shade trees. The time is around noon in early summer.

The words LAST DAY OF SCHOOL are gradually scrawled across the blackboard.

CUT TO:

Three Girls Near Bay Window:
Virginia McCoo (polio cripple, sharp features, strident voice); Phyllis Chatfield (chubby, sturdy); and a third girl (head turned away, tying her shoe).

VIRGINIA   (*to Phyllis*) Well, Phyllis, what are your plans for the summer? Camp?

PHYLLIS   Yes, camp. My folks are going to Europe.

VIRGINIA   Getting rid of you, huh?

PHYLLIS   Oh well, I don't mind. I like camp.

VIRGINIA   Same place—Lake Climax?

PHYLLIS   Same old place. And what about you, Ginny?

VIRGINIA   I'm going to have a wonderful time. I'm going to have French lessons with our new paying guest.

PHYLLIS   Oh—has he come?

VIRGINIA   Coming tomorrow. My mother saw him in New York and she says he's a real man of the world and awfully handsome. I guess it will be fun.

PHYLLIS   (*to the third girl*) And you, Lolita?

Lolita turns toward them. A smile, a shrug.

CUT TO:

A Car Drives up to the School. Charlotte Haze Emerges.

LOLITA   There's my dear mother.

CUT TO:

A Teacher Coming out meets Charlotte Coming in.

TEACHER   How are you, Mrs. Haze?

CHARLOTTE   Fine. And you, Miss Horton—glad to be rid of them until the fall?

TEACHER   I should say so. Now it's Mama's turn to take over. Is Lolita going to the Lake Climax camp?

CHARLOTTE   I don't know. I sort of never got around to planning our summer yet.

CUT TO:

Charlotte Drives Lolita Homeward.
Heavy traffic. Red light.

LOLITA   Our luck as per usual. (*Pause.*)

Light changes

    With our luck it is sure to be some ugly old hag.

CHARLOTTE   What are you talking about?

LOLITA   About the lodger you are trying to find.

CHARLOTTE   Oh, *that*. Well, I'm sure she will be a lovely person. When the time comes. The agency tells me it is going to be quite a season here this summer. What with the new casino.

LOLITA   Ginny McCoo was telling me about the roomer *they* are getting. He's a professor of French poetry. And her uncle's firm is going to publish a book he has written.

CHARLOTTE   We don't want any French poets. *Please*, stop rummaging in that glove compartment.

LOLITA   I had some candy there.

CHARLOTTE   You are wrecking your teeth on those mints. By the way, you have not forgotten you have Dr. Quilty at three and—oh, darn that dog!

CUT TO:

Mr. Jung's Dog, a Large Collie,
waits at the corner of Lawn Street, then races the car barking
lustily and nearly gets run over.

CHARLOTTE   Really, I am fed up with that beast.

CUT TO:

She Draws up at the Curb
where old Mr. Jung is inspecting the contents of his mailbox.
Over his spectacles he peers at Mrs. Haze.

CHARLOTTE   (*leaning out*) Mr. Jung, something
     must be done about that dog of yours.

Mr. Jung, beaming and a little gaga, walks around the car to
her window.

CUT TO:

Lolita, leaning out of her side of the car,
fondly stroking the pleased hound and speaking confidentially—

LOLITA   And I think he is a good, good dog—yes, a
     good dog.

CUT TO:

Mr. Jung, who is a little deaf
and seems to listen with his mouth, comes closer to the driver's
window.

CHARLOTTE   I am talking about your dog. Something
     must be done about him.

MR. JUNG   Why? What's he been up to?

CHARLOTTE   He's a nuisance. He chases every car. He has taught two other dogs to do it.

MR. JUNG   He's a gentle intelligent beast. Never hurt anybody. Most alert and intelligent.

CHARLOTTE   I'm not interested in his I.Q. All I know he's a nuisance. And it will be your fault if he gets hurt.

MR. JUNG   He won't hurt nobody. Come here, boy! You just don't mind him, Mrs. Haze. Come, boy!

LOLITA   Mother, I'm hungry. Let's be moving.

WIPE TO:

Dinner Time.
Quick view of Ramsdale. White church with clock against an inky sky. Lolita dines from a plate watching TV.

DISSOLVE TO:

A Ragged Sunset.
The plashing lake. A thunderhead looming.

Details of approaching electric storm: an empty milk bottle overturned by a gust.

The wind brutally turns the pages of the mangled magazine forgotten on the folding chair. It is suddenly whisked away in rotating mad flight.

Nightfall. Lolita barefooted hastens to close a bedroom window. Lightning. Charlotte folds and drags in the garden chair. The thunder claps and rolls. Another flash.

CUT TO:

LOLITA   (*undressed, on landing, to her mother downstairs*) I'm going to bed. I'm scared!

Big Thunderclap

CUT TO:

Charlotte in the Living Room.
The storm never stops. Far away the fire engine is heard. Nearer. Far again. Charlotte looks out of the window. Details of nocturnal storm: gesticulating black trees, rain drumming on roof, thunder, lightning printing reflections on wall, Lolita sits up in bed. More sounds of firefighting.

CUT TO:

A Car,
shedding its moving beam on 342 Lawn Street, and then on 345 Lawn Street, turns in to the driveway next door. The Farlows, John and Jean. The storm is abating.

JEAN   John, while you are parking the car I'll dash over to Charlotte and tell her——

JOHN   Oh, but she must be fast asleep.

JEAN   No, she's in the living room. The lights are on.

CUT TO:

[26]

Charlotte, Who has noticed their return, opens the front door. A cat's eyes in the dripping-dark. Sheet lightning.

JEAN   Oh, what's that cat doing there? Have you heard about the fire, Charlotte?

CHARLOTTE   I heard the engines.

JEAN   Well, it was at the McCoos'.

CHARLOTTE   No!

JEAN   Yes. Their house got struck by lightning. We were at John's club and could see the blaze five blocks away.

CHARLOTTE   My goodness! Are they safe?

JEAN   Oh yes, they're okay. They even saved the TV. But the house is practically a burnt-out shell.

CHARLOTTE   But how *dreadful!*

JEAN   Naturally they were insured and all that—and they have that apartment in Parkington. Well, see you tomorrow. Bye-bye.

CUT TO:

Early Morning Next Day.
Robin pulling out worm on damp lawn. One new dandelion. Milkman collects empty bottles. Tinkle. Telephone takes over, rings.

Lolita in pajamas, barefoot, leaning over banisters, half a story above Charlotte, who attends to the telephone in the hallway. The conversation is nearing its end. We hear only her side.

CHARLOTTE   I certainly could, Mr. McCoo. Oh, I just keep thinking and thinking of you and that dreadful fire——

(*Listens.*)

No trouble at all. In fact it's just the kind of lodger——

(*Listens.*)

Yes, I see. Yes, of course.

(*Listens.*)

Well, I'm glad he's old-fashioned enough to prefer lakes to oceans. That means a quiet lodger.

(*Laughs demurely.*)
(*Listens.*)

Oh, I could fetch him if you'd like.

(*Listens.*)

I see.

(*Listens.*)

Look, why don't you meet him at the station, explain things to him, put him into Joe's taxi, and send him over here.

[28]

(Listens.)

Aha. Naturally. I understand that.

(Listens.)

Okay then. I'll be expecting him around noon.

(Listens.)

Not at all, not at all *(melodious laugh)*. Everything in the world happens at short notice.

(Listens.)

Yes, do that. You know, I could not sleep all night thinking of that dreadful fire and your poor wife. You're so right to have sent her and Ginny to Parkington. Well, please do tell your wife that if there's anything I can do——

(Hangs up.)

LOLITA   Mother, is that man going to stay with us?

CHARLOTTE   He is. Oh dear, Louise is not coming until after tomorrow. You had better get dressed and pick up all those books and things you brought back from school. The hall is a mess.

CUT TO:

Humbert's Arrival

FADE IN

Ramsdale (a thriving resort, somewhere between Minnesota and Maine)
as seen by a traveler arriving by plane. We are served the dish of the large, pine-fringed, scintillating Ramsdale Lake, with, at one end, a recreation park and a stucco pleasure dome. A small cloud of dark smoke is hanging over part of the suburban development. Beyond this is the cheerful, neat-looking town in the sunshine of a serene May morning. The airport spreads out beneath us, flying its flags and gently gyrating as the plane's shadow sweeps over it.

CUT TO:

Alfalfa Fields, Asphalted Spaces, Parked Cars: Ramsdale Airport
Humbert carrying briefcase lands and enters the office. His bags follow. He looks around.

HUMBERT   Somebody was supposed to meet me. . . .

He consults a little black diary.

DESK CLERK   Can I help you, sir?

HUMBERT   May I use this phone?

He attempts to dial McCoo's number. Consults his diary again. Redials. There is no answer.

HUMBERT   Funny. (*to the clerk*) Where can I find
    a taxi?

CLERK   (*pointing with pencil*) Down there. He'll take
    your bags.

CUT TO:

Humbert in Taxi
They cross the town and turn in to Lake Avenue. Sounds of fire engines. Firefighters going back to their station.

TAXI DRIVER We sure had a big storm last night. Lightning struck a house in Lake Avenue, and oh boy, did it burn!
(*does a double take*)
Say, mister, what number you said you were going?

HUMBERT Nine hundred. Nine oh oh.

TAXI DRIVER (*chuckling*) Well, "oh-oh" is about all that's left of it.

CUT TO:

The Black, Hosewater-drenched, Still Smoking Remains of a Burned-Down House
Policemen are still keeping away a thinning crowd of spectators, most of whom have come by car or bicycle. The·charred ruins are those of the McCoo villa in a pine-treed, sparsely populated part of Lake Avenue. Humbert's taxi stops at a roped-off puddle.

TAXI DRIVER (*continuously indulging in raw, ready humor*) Here you are, sir.

HUMBERT My goodness! You mean this is the McCoo residence?

TAXI DRIVER Residence? Oh, brother!

Humbert, automatically carrying raincoat and briefcase, climbs out of the car. Faint cheers from the crowd.

PATROLMAN   You can't come any closer.

HUMBERT   I'm supposed to live here.

PATROLMAN   Why don't you speak to the owner? That's Mr. McCoo down there.

(In the following scene the grotesque humor turns upon McCoo's conducting a kind of guided tour through a non-existent house. He makes the belated honors of the home Humbert would have shared.) McCoo, a small fat man, emerges from the ruins of the patio. He staggers along with a big barbecue roaster in his arms. He is dirty and wet, and utterly bewildered. He stops and stares at Humbert.

HUMBERT   How do you do. I am your lodger. Or rather I was to be your lodger.

McCOO   (*setting down his burden*) What do you know! Mr. Humbert, I must apologize. I thought my wife would leave you a message at the airport. I know she found other lodgings for you. Look at this dreadful disaster.

He gestures toward architectural ghosts in the aura of the vanished villa.

McCOO   Follow me. Look, sir, look. Your room was right here. A beautiful, sunny, quiet studio. That was your bed—with a brand-new mattress. Here you had a writing desk—you see, that's where the wall ran—where that hose lies now.

[32]

Humbert blankly considers a heap of water-soaked volumes.

McCOO   Ginny's encyclopedia. (*Glances up at a non-existent upper story.*) Must have dropped through the floor of my daughter's room. Good illustrations. Cathedrals. Cocoa Industry. It's a wonder that bolt did not kill Mrs. McCoo and me in the master bedroom. Our little daughter was quite hysterical. Oh, it was such a lovely home. A regular showpiece. People came all the way from Parkington to see it.

Humbert stumbles over a board.

McCOO   Careful. I know there is not much left but I'd like you to see the patio. Here was the barbecue table. Well, that's all out now. I had planned to have you give lessons in French to my little Ginny, the poor pet. I've bundled them off to Parkington. And of course I'm fully insured. But still it's a terrible shock. Now, about that other place for you——

McCoo, wiping a dirty face with a dirty hand, walks back to the street with carefully high-stepping Humbert. The camera escorts them.

McCOO   We thought that other place would be the best arrangement, under these sad circumstances. We all have to rough it now. She's a widow, a delightful personality with a lot of culture. But it's not as grand as here, though much nearer to town. The address is 342 Lawn Street. Let me direct your taxi. Hullo, Joe.

CUT TO:

Hysterical Bark of a car-chasing *Collie* on Lawn Street, down which Humbert's taxi arrives to stop at No. 342, an unattractive white clapboard suburban house, with a smooth philistine lawn where only one dandelion has survived the leveling power mower. Humbert emerges, watched by Charlotte from an upper window. The driver is about to help with the suitcases.

HUMBERT   No, leave those bags. I want you to wait a few minutes.

DRIVER   Sure.

HUMBERT   I doubt very much that I'll stay here. (*in vocal brackets*) What a horrible house.

The door is ajar. Humbert enters. The hallway is graced with Mexican knicknacks and the banal favorites of arty middle-class (such as a Van Gogh reproduction). An old tennis racket with a broken string lies on an oak chest. There is a telephone on a small table near the living-room door, which is ajar.

From the upper landing comes the voice of Mrs. Haze, who leans over the banisters inquiring melodiously: "Is that Monsieur Humbert?"

A bit of cigarette ash drops from above as Humbert looks up. Presently the lady herself—sandals, slacks, silk blouse, Marlenesque face (in that order)—comes down the steps, her index finger still tapping upon the cigarette.

Shake hands.

HUMBERT   How do you do. Allow me to explain the situation.

CHARLOTTE   Yes—I know everything. Come on in.

CUT TO:

Humbert and Charlotte enter the parlor
She makes Javanese-like gestures: inviting him to choose a seat.
(N.B.: these gestures will be repeated by Dolly Schiller in
last scene of play). They sit down.

CHARLOTTE   Let's get acquainted and then I'll show
   you your room. I have only Dromes.

HUMBERT   Thanks, I don't smoke.

CHARLOTTE   Oh well, one vice the less. I'm a tissue
   of little vices. *C'est la vie.* (*Lights up.*) You're sure
   you're comfortable in that old chair?

He removes from under his thigh an old tennis ball.

HUMBERT   Oh, perfectly.

CHARLOTTE   (*relieving him of the ball*) I think, Mr.
   Humbert, I have exactly what you are looking for. I
   understand you wanted to stay at Ramsdale all summer?

HUMBERT   I'm not sure. No, I really could not say.
   The point is I have been very ill, and a friend suggested
   Ramsdale. I imagined a spacious house on the shore of
   a lake.

The CAMERA meanwhile examines ironically various cran-
nies of the room.

CHARLOTTE   Well, the lake is only two miles from
   my spacious house.

HUMBERT   Oh, I know. But I envisaged a villa, white dunes, the accessible ripples, a system of morning dips.

CHARLOTTE   Frankly, between you and I, the McCoo residence, though perhaps a bit more modern than mine, is not at all on the lake front, not at all. You have to walk two blocks to see it.

HUMBERT   Oh, I'm sure there would have been some flaw, some disappointment. What I mean is that I was pursuing a particular dream, not *any* house but *that* house.

CHARLOTTE   I'm sorry for the McCoos—but they should not have promised too much. Well, I can offer you congenial surroundings in a very select neighborhood. If you like golf, as I am sure you do, we are practically at walking distance from the country club. And we are very intellectual, yes sir. You are a professor of poetry, aren't you?

HUMBERT   Alas. I shall be teaching at Beardsley College next year.

CHARLOTTE   Then you will certainly want to address our club, of which I am a proud member. Last time we had Professor Amy King, a very stimulating teacher type, talk to us on Dr. Schweitzer and Dr. Zhivago. Now let us take a peek at that room. I'm positive you're going to love it.

CUT TO:

Charlotte and Humbert reach the upper landing

CHARLOTTE   It's what you might call a semi-studio—
or *almost* a semi-studio.

She closes quickly the door to Lolita's room, which is ajar,
and opens a door opposite.

CHARLOTTE   Well here we are. Isn't that a cute book-
shelf? Look at those colonial book ends. Now, in that
corner (*meditative pause, with elbow in palm*) I shall
put our spare radio set.

HUMBERT   No, no. Please, no radio.

He winces as he glances at a picture: a reproduction of René
Prinet's "Kreutzer Sonata"—the unappetizing one in which
a disheveled violinist passionately embraces his fair accompa-
nist as she rises from her piano stool with clammy young
hands still touching the keys.

CHARLOTTE   Now, that's a rug Mr. Haze and I bought
in Mexico. We went there on our honeymoon, which
was—let me see—thirteen years ago.

HUMBERT   Which was about the time I got married.

CHARLOTTE   Oh, you are married?

HUMBERT   Divorced, madam, happily divorced.

CHARLOTTE   Where was that? In Europe?

HUMBERT   In Paris.

CHARLOTTE   Paris must be wonderful at this time of
the year. As a matter of fact, we were planning a trip to

Europe just before Mr. Haze died, after three years of great happiness. He was a lovely person, a man of complete integrity. I know you would have enjoyed talking to him and he to you. Now, here we have——

Humbert opens a closet. A painted screen of the folding type topples into his arms. Pictured on it is a nymphet in three repeated designs: (1) gazing over a black gauze fan, (2) in a black half-mask, (3) in bikini and harlequin glasses. There is a rent in the fabric.

CHARLOTTE   Oops! I *am* sorry. We bought it at the store here to match our Mexican stuff but it did not wear well. I'll have Lolita remove it to her room. She loves it.

HUMBERT   You have a maid living in the house?

CHARLOTTE   Oh no, what do you think? Ramsdale is not Paris. There's a colored girl who comes three times a week and we think we're lucky to have her. I see this bed-lamp does not work. I'll have it fixed.

HUMBERT   But I thought you said——

Carefully and rather wistfully, Charlotte closes the door of the unsuccessful room. She opens another door next to it.

CHARLOTTE   This is the bathroom. I'm sure that as a European intellectual you hate our luxurious modern monstrosities—tiled tubs and goldern faucets. This here is a good old-fashioned type with the kind of quaint plumbing that should appeal to an Englishman. I must apologize for this dirty sock. Now, if we walk down again I'll show you the dining room—and, of course, my beautiful garden.

HUMBERT   I understood there would be a private bath.

CHARLOTTE   Sorry.

HUMBERT   I don't want to take so much of your time. It must be a frightful bother——

CHARLOTTE   No bother at all.

Humbert and Charlotte walk via the parlor into the dining room, the camera trucking with them.

CHARLOTTE   Here we have our meals. Down there is the sun porch. Well, that's about all, *cher Monsieur.*
(*sigh*)
I'm afraid you are not too favorably impressed.

HUMBERT   I must think it over. I have a taxi waiting out there. Let me take down your telephone number.

CHARLOTTE   Ramsdale 1776. So easy to remember. I won't charge you much, you know. Two hundred per month, all meals included.

HUMBERT   I see. Didn't I have a raincoat?

CHARLOTTE   I saw you leave it in the car.

HUMBERT   So I did. Well——

He bows.

CHARLOTTE   Oh, but you *must* visit my garden!

Humbert follows her.

CHARLOTTE   That's the kitchen there. You might like to know I'm a very good cook. My pastries win prizes round here.

Humbert follows Charlotte to the veranda. Now comes the shock of dazzling enchantment and recognition. "From a mat in a pool of sun, half-naked, kneeling turning about on her knees, my Riviera love was peering at me over dark glasses."

It might be a good idea at this point to film the extended metaphor of the next paragraph: "As if I were the fairy-tale nurse of some little princess—lost, kidnapped, discovered in Gypsy rags through which her nakedness smiled at the king and his hounds, I recognized the tiny dark-brown mole on her side." Humbert, much disturbed, follows Charlotte down into the garden.

CHARLOTTE   That was my daughter, and these are my lilies.

HUMBERT   (*mumbling*) Beautiful, beautiful....

CHARLOTTE   (*with winsome abandon*) Well, this is all I can offer you—a comfortable home, a sunny garden, my lilies, my Lolita, my cherry pies.

HUMBERT   Yes, yes. I'm very grateful. You said fifty per week, including meals?

CHARLOTTE   So you *are* going to stay with us?

HUMBERT   Why—yes. I'd like to move in right now.

CHARLOTTE   You dear man. That's wonderful. Was my garden the decisive factor?

CUT TO:

Veranda where Lolita, in briefs and bra, is sunning herself on the mat
Charlotte and Humbert returning to the house mount the steps from the garden.

CHARLOTTE   I'll pay your taxi and have the luggage put in your room. Do you have many things?

HUMBERT   There's a briefcase and a typewriter, and a tape recorder, and a raincoat. And two suitcases. May I——

CHARLOTTE   No, it's okay. I know from Mrs. McCoo that you are not supposed to carry things.

HUMBERT   Oh yes, and there's also a box of chocolates I intended to bring the McCoos.

Charlotte smiles and exits.

LOLITA   Yum-yum.

HUMBERT   So you are Lolita.

LOLITA   Yes, that's me.

Turns from sea-star supine to seal prone. There is a pause.

HUMBERT   It's a beautiful day.

LOLITA   Very.

HUMBERT   (*sitting down on the steps*) Nice here. Oh, the floor is hot.

[41]

LOLITA (*Pushes a cushion toward him.*) Make yourself comfortable.

She is now in a half-sitting position.

LOLITA Did you see the fire?

HUMBERT No, it was all over when I came. Poor Mr. McCoo looked badly shaken.

LOLITA You look badly shaken yourself.

HUMBERT Why, no. I'm all right. I suppose I should change into lighter clothes. There's a ladybird on your leg.

LOLITA It's a ladybug, not a ladybird.

She transfers it to her finger and attempts to coax it into flight.

HUMBERT You should blow. Like this. There she goes.

LOLITA Ginny McCoo—she's in my class, you know. And she said you were going to be her tutor.

HUMBERT Oh, that's greatly exaggerated. The idea was I might help her with her French.

LOLITA She's grim, Ginny.

HUMBERT Is she—well, attractive?

LOLITA She's a fright. And mean. And lame.

HUMBERT Really? That's curious. Lame?

LOLITA   Yah. She had polio or something. Are you going to help me with my homework?

HUMBERT   *Mais oui*, Lolita. *Aujourd'hui?*

Charlotte comes in.

CHARLOTTE   That's where you are.

LOLITA   He's going to help me with my homework.

CHARLOTTE   Fine. Mr. Humbert, I paid your taxi and had the man take your things upstairs. You owe me four dollars thirty-five. Later, later. Dolores, I think Mr. Humbert would like to rest.

HUMBERT   Oh no, I'll help her with pleasure.

Charlotte leaves.

LOLITA   Well, there's not much today. Gee, school will be over in three weeks.

A pause.

HUMBERT   May I—I want to pluck some tissue paper out of that box. No, you're lying on it. There—let me—thanks.

LOLITA   Hold on. This bit has my lipstick on it.

HUMBERT   Does your mother allow lipstick?

LOLITA   She does not. I hide it here.

She indraws her pretty abdomen and produces the lipstick from under the band of her shorts.

HUMBERT   You're a very amusing little girl. Do you often go to the lake shore? I shaw—I mean, I saw that beautiful lake from the plane.

LOLITA   (*lying back with a sigh*) Almost never. It's quite a way. And my mummy's too lazy to go there with me. Besides, we kids prefer the town pool.

HUMBERT   Who is your favorite recording star?

LOLITA   Oh, I dunno.

HUMBERT   What grade are you in?

LOLITA   This a quiz?

HUMBERT   I only want to know more about you. I know that you like to solarize your solar plexus. But what else do you like?

LOLITA   You shouldn't use such words, you know.

HUMBERT   Should I say "what you *dig*"?

LOLITA   That's old hat.

Pause. Lolita turns over on her tummy. Humbert, awkwardly squatting, tense, twitching, mutely moaning, devours her with sad eyes; Lolita, a restless sunbather, sits up again.

HUMBERT   Is there anything special you'd like to be when you grow up?

LOLITA   What?

HUMBERT   I said——

Lolita, eyes shuttling, listens to the telephone ringing in the remote hallway and to her mother attending to it.

LOLITA   (*yelling*) Mother, is it for me?

HUMBERT   I said what would you like to be?

Charlotte enters from dining room. Humbert, interrupted in his furtive lust, scrambles up guiltily.

CHARLOTTE   It's Kenny. I suspect he wants to escort you to the big dance next month.

Lolita, groping, skipping on one foot, half-shod, shedding beach slipper, whirling, taking off, bumping into humid Humbert, laughing, exits barefoot.

CHARLOTTE   I'll be driving downtown in a few minutes. Like me to take you somewhere? Like to see Ramsdale?

HUMBERT   First I'd like to change. I never thought it would be so warm in Ramsdale.

CUT TO:

Humbert's Room. A few days have elapsed.
Humbert jots down last night's dream: A somewhat ripply shot reveals: a knight in full armor riding a black horse along a forest road. Three nymphets, one lame, are playing in a sun-shot glade. Nymphet Lolita runs toward Humbert, the

Dark Knight, and promptly seats herself behind. His visor closes again. At a walking pace they ride deeper into the Enchanted Forest.

DISSOLVE TO NEXT ENTRY:

We are on the piazza. Humbert takes up a strategic position in rocker, with voluminous Sunday paper, in the vicinity of two parallel mats. He rocks and feigns to read. Exaggerate the volume of the paper.

Mother and daughter, both in two-piece bathing suits, come to sun themselves.

CUT TO:

Charlotte transposes jar of skin cream from farther mat (mat 2) to nearer mat (mat 1) and sits down on mat 1. Lolita yanks the comics section, and the family section, and the magazine section out of Humbert's paper and makes herself comfortable on mat 2.

There is an area of shade beyond her. Into this area Humbert, the furtive writer, gently rocking arrives in his ambling chair. He is now near Lolita.

Mother, far, supine, on mat 1 (now the farthest) lavishly anointed, exhibits herself to the sun; daughter, near, prone, on mat 2, showing Humbert her narrow nates and the seaside of her thighs, is immersed in the funnies.

Tenderly, the rocker rocks.
A mourning dove coos.

Charlotte gropes for her cigarettes but they are on mat 2, nearer to Humbert. She half rises and transfers herself to a new position, between him and her daughter, whom she shoves onto mat 1.

Charlotte, now on mat 2, near Humbert, fusses with lighter and casts a look at what he is grimly perusing: book review, a full-page ad:

WHEN THE LILACS LAST

most controversial novel of the year, 300,000 copies in print.

CHARLOTTE   Have you read that? *When the Lilacs Last.*

Humbert (*Clears his throat negatively.*)

CHARLOTTE   Oh, you should. It was given a rave review by Adam Scott. It's about a man from the North and a girl from the South who build up a beautiful relationship—he is her father image and she is his mother image, but later she discovers that as a child she had rejected her father, and of course then he begins to identify her with his possessive mother. You see, it works out this way: he symbolizes the industrial North, and she symbolizes the old-fashioned South, and——

LOLITA   (*casually*) and it's all silly nonsense.

CHARLOTTE   Dolores Haze, will you go up to your room at once.

THREE WEEKS LATER, THE DAY OF THE SCHOOL DANCE.

FADE IN:

Kitchen—the Cat and the Morning Milk are let in
Charlotte, dainty-aproned, prepares breakfast for Humbert. He enters, wearing a silk jacket with frogs.

HUMBERT   Good morning.

He sits down at the breakfast-niche table. Puts his elbows
on it and meditates.

CHARLOTTE   Your bacon is ready.

Humbert considers the calendar on the wall and reaches into
his back pocket for his wallet.

HUMBERT   My fourth week starts today.

CHARLOTTE   The time certainly flies. Monsieur is
    served.

HUMBERT   Fifty, and the eight twenty I owe you for
    the wine.

CHARLOTTE   No, it's sixty-two thirty-five: I paid for
    the *Glance* subscription, remember?

HUMBERT   Oh, I thought I had settled that.

He settles.

CHARLOTTE   Well, today is the big party. I bet she'll
    be pestering me all morning with her dance dress.

HUMBERT   Isn't that rather normal?

CHARLOTTE   Oh, yes. Definitely. I am all for these
    formal affairs. It may suggest to the hoyden she is some
    elements of gracious living.
        (*Sits down at the table.*)

On the other hand—this is the end of that blessed era, school year. After which we'll be in for a period of slouching, disorganized boredom, vehement griping, feigned gagging, and all the rest of it.

HUMBERT   Hm. Aren't you exaggerating a bit?

CHARLOTTE   Oh, I leave *that* to her. Exaggerating is all hers. How I hate that diffused clowning—what they call "goofing off." In *my* day, which after all was only a couple of short decades ago, I never indulged in that sprawling, droopy, dopy-eyed style.

Lolita's voice is heard calling from the stairs.

CHARLOTTE   (*making a grimace of resignation*) See what I mean?
                                        (*to Lolita*)
Yes? What is it?

LOLITA   (*carrying a slip*) You promised to fix this.

CHARLOTTE   Okay. Later.

LOLITA   (*to Humbert*) Well: coming to our hop?

CHARLOTTE   My daughter means: Do you intend to attend her school dance.

HUMBERT   I understood. Yes, thank you.

CHARLOTTE   We parents are not supposed to dance, of course.

LOLITA   What do you mean "we"?

CHARLOTTE   (*flustered*) Oh, I mean adults. Parents and their friends.

Lolita exits singing.

HUMBERT   When does it start?

CHARLOTTE   Around four. I have some nice cold chicken for you afterwards.
                (*seeing him rise*)
Back to Baudelaire?

HUMBERT   Yes. I wanted to write in the garden but our neighbor's gardener has again set loose his motor mower or whatever you call it. It's deafening and sickening.

CHARLOTTE   I always think of it as an exhilarating, cheerful kind of sound. It brings back heaps of green summers and that kind of thing.

HUMBERT   You Americans are immune to noise.

CHARLOTTE   Anyway, Lesley stops work at noon, and you'll have lots of time before the party.

CUT TO:

The Garden
Humbert in the leafy shade, writes in his little black book. Mourning doves moan, cicadas whirr, a jet beyond sight and sound leaves its twin wakelines of silvery chalk in the cloudless sky. A mother's voice is heard calling somewhere up the street: "Rosy! Ro-sy!" It is a very pleasant afternoon. Humbert consults his watch and glances up at the house. He gets

up and strolls around, quietly trying to locate Lolita, whose voice is heard now in one room, now in another, while radio music comes from a third. Presently the bath water is heard performing, filling the tub, and then emptying into the drain. Humbert assembles his papers and walks to the house.

CUT TO:

The Living Room
Humbert feigning to read a magazine. Lolita swishes into the room wearing a pale billowy-skirted dance dress and pale satin pumps. She gracefully gyrates in front of Humbert.

LOLITA   Well? Do you like me?

HUMBERT   (*a phony judge*) Very much.

LOLITA   Adoration? Beauty in the mist? Too dreamy for words?

HUMBERT   I am often amazed at your verbal felicity, Lolita.

LOLITA   Check my back zipper, will you?

HUMBERT   There's some talc on your shoulder blades. May I remove it?

LOLITA   It depends.

HUMBERT   There.

LOLITA   Silly boy.

HUMBERT   I am three times your age.

LOLITA   Tell it to Mom.

HUMBERT   Why?

LOLITA   Oh, I guess you tell her everything.

HUMBERT   Wait a minute, Lolita. Don't waltz. A great poet said: Stop, moment———. You are beautiful.

LOLITA   (*feigning to call*) Mother!

HUMBERT   Even when you play the fool.

LOLITA   That's not English.

HUMBERT   It's English enough for me.

LOLITA   D'you think this dress will make Kenny gulp?

HUMBERT   Who's Kenny?

LOLITA   He's my date for tonight. Jealous?

HUMBERT   In fact, yes.

LOLITA   Delirious? Dolly-mad?

HUMBERT   Yes, yes. Oh, wait!

LOLITA   And she flew away.

She flies away.

CUT TO:

The Landing
Humbert in a flannel suit and Charlotte in a glamorous gown (from Rosenthal, The Rose of Ramsdale, 50 South Main Street).

HUMBERT   Are we supposed to pick up her young man?

CHARLOTTE   No. He said he'd call for her. He lives two blocks from here. I'll bet she'll be prettying herself up to the last moment.

CUT TO:

The Driveway, Facing the Garage
Kenny helps Lolita to get into the back of the Haze two-door sedan. On the other side Humbert opens the driver's door for Charlotte. Daughter and Mother settle down with the same preenings, the same rhythm of rustle and rerustle. Humbert starts walking around the car. Charlotte turns to Kenny, who is about to join Lolita.

CHARLOTTE   It's the new building, isn't it?

KENNY   Yes, ma'am.

CHARLOTTE   And Chestnut Street is closed for repairs?

KENNY   Yes. You have to turn after the church.

CHARLOTTE   Church? I thought it was the other way. Let me see—

LOLITA   Look, Kenny, why don't you get in beside Mother and direct her?

CHARLOTTE   Don't bother. I'll find it.

LOLITA   No, you won't. Please, Ken. And you come here.

Pats the seat next to her for Hum. Humbert, not without hitting his head against the lintel, climbs in and arranges his long limbs beside Lolita's bouffant skirt. The backrest of the passenger seat is pushed into place by Kenny who briskly seats himself next to Charlotte. She gives vent to her irritation by getting into reverse gear so abruptly that Lolita's purse leaps off her lap. Lolita and Humbert fumble for it.

LOLITA   (*laughing*) Easy, Mother.

CHARLOTTE   (*controlling herself*) No backseat driving, children.

And that is how Humbert obtains a few minutes of secret alliance with the nymphet. Deliberately, Lolita lets her hand rest on his, lets it slip into his, be enveloped by his.

CUT TO:

The New Hall
School punch and cookies are served in the gallery where teachers, parents, and their friends stand around in more or less garrulous groups. *Music* comes from the adjacent room, where the children are dancing. Charlotte introduces Humbert to the Chatfields.

CHARLOTTE   Ann, I want you to meet Professor Humbert, who is staying with us. Mrs. Chatfield, Mr. Chatfield.

How do you do's are exchanged.

MRS. CHATFIELD   (*to Charlotte*) Your Lolita looks perfectly enchanting in that cloud of pink. And the way she moves. . . . Oh, my!

CHARLOTTE   Thank you. And I was about to compliment you on your Phyllis. She's a darling. I understand you are sending her to the Climax Lake camp next week?

MRS. CHATFIELD   Yes. It's the healthiest place in the world. Run by a remarkable woman who believes in natural education. Which, of course, is progressive education combined with nature.

CHARLOTTE   Say, who is that gentleman in the fancy waistcoat whom those women are mobbing? He looks familiar to me.

MRS. CHATFIELD   Oh, Charlotte! That's Clare Quilty, the playwright.

CHARLOTTE   Of course. I quite forgot that our good old dentist had such a distinguished nephew. Didn't you adore his play which they had on the TV, *The Nymphet?*

CUT TO:

Another Part of the Gallery
In the meantime, after some dreary small talk with Mr. Chatfield (Chatfield: I hear, Professor, you're going to teach at Beardsley College. I believe the wife of our president—I work for the Lakewood corporation—majored there in Home Economics.), Humbert drifts away. He wanders toward the dance floor and watches Lolita. The second or third slow dance has terminated and now a more boisterous strain hits the ear-

drum. Kenny and Lolita go through an energetic rock 'n' roll. Humbert leans his shoulder against a pillar. The camera picks out his Adam's apple.

CUT TO:

The Refreshments Table Near Which Charlotte Stands
She casts a questing look around. She has lost Humbert. Two gigglers in full skirts rustle past rapidly, heading for the ballroom.

FIRST GIRL   (*to second*) D'you know who that was? Clare Quilty! Oh, gosh, I got a real bang out of seeing him.

Charlotte's roving eye meets the gaze of the English teacher, Miss Adams, in the Quilty group. Miss Adams beckons to her. Charlotte floats thither. Introductions. Quilty is a tremendously successful phony, fortyish, roguish, baldish, with an obscene little mustache and a breezy manner which some find insulting and others just love.

CHARLOTTE   Oh, but I have met Mr. Quilty before.
(*Elegantly appropriates him.*)
Mr. Quilty, I'm a great fan of yours.

QUILTY   Ah yes—ah yes——

CHARLOTTE   We met two years ago——

QUILTY   (*ironically purring*) An eternity——

CHARLOTTE   We had that luncheon in your honor at the club——

[56]

QUILTY   I can imagine it better than I recall it——

CHARLOTTE   And afterwards I showed you my garden and drove you to the airport——

QUILTY   Ah yes—magnificent airport.

He attempts to leave her orbit.

CHARLOTTE   Are you here for some time?

QUILTY   Oh, very briefly. Came to borrow a little cash from Uncle Ivor. Excuse me, I think I must go now. They are putting on a play of mine in Parkington.

CHARLOTTE   Recently we had the pleasure of enjoying your *Nymphet* on Channel 5.

QUILTY   Great fun those channels. Well, it was a joy chatting about the past.

He moves away sidling into the crowd but stops suddenly and turns.

QUILTY   Say, didn't you have a little girl? Let me see. With a lovely name. A lovely lilting lyrical name——

CHARLOTTE   Lolita. Diminutive of Dolores.

QUILTY   Ah, of course: Dolores. The tears and the roses.

CHARLOTTE   She's dancing down there. And tomorrow she'll be having a cavity filled by your uncle.

QUILTY   I know; he's a wicked old man.

MISS ADAMS   Mr. Quilty, I'm afraid I must tear you away. There's somebody come from Parkington to fetch you.

QUILTY   They can wait. I want to watch Dolores dance.

CUT TO:

Gallery Near Refreshments
Humbert appears.

CHARLOTTE   Where have you been all this time?

HUMBERT   Just strolling around.

CHARLOTTE   You look bored stiff, you poor man. Oh, hullo, Emily.

MRS. GRAY   Good evening, Charlotte.

CHARLOTTE   Emily, this is Professor Humbert, who is staying with us. Mrs. Gray.

Handshakes

MRS. GRAY   Isn't it a lovely party?

CHARLOTTE   Is your darling Rose having a good time?

MRS. GRAY   Oh, yes. You know, that child is insatiable. She got some new records for her birthday, so she plans to dance to them with Jack Beale and a couple of other kids after the party. She'd like to ask Lolita and Kenny. Could Lolita go with us from here? I'll give her supper.

CHARLOTTE   By all means. That's a delightful arrangement.

MRS. GRAY   Wonderful. I'll bring her back. Around ten?

CHARLOTTE   Make it eleven. Thank you very much, Emily.

Mrs. Gray joins another group.

CHARLOTTE (*taking Humbert's arm*) And *we* can go home and have a nice cozy supper. Is that all right with you, *cher monsieur*?

CUT TO:

The Haze Living Room
Charlotte and Humbert have finished their cold chicken and salad and are now sipping liqueurs in the parlor.

CHARLOTTE   I consider crème de menthe to be the supremely divine nectar. This was given me by the Farlows. Cost them a small fortune, I suspect.

Humbert eyes casually a diminutive circular sticker with the price "$2.50." They clink and drink.

CHARLOTTE   Well—*votre santé*. Now let's have some good music.

Humbert looks at his wristwatch, and then at the clock.

CHARLOTTE   Bartók or Bardinski?

HUMBERT   Doesn't matter—Bardinski, rather. I am not at all sure that those parties are properly chaperoned.

CHARLOTTE   What parties? What are you talking about?

HUMBERT   Parties at the homes of mothers. Record-playing sessions in the basement with the lights out.

CHARLOTTE   Oh, that! Really, Mr. Humbert, I have more exciting things to think about than the manners of modern children. Look, let's change the subject. I mean, after all . . . can't we forget my tedious daughter? Here's a proposal: why don't I teach you some of the new dance steps? What say you?

HUMBERT   I don't even know the old ones. I'm an awkward tripper and have no sense of rhythm.

CHARLOTTE   Oh, come on. Come on, Humbert. May I call you Humbert? Especially as nobody can tell which it is of your two names? Or do you think the surname is pronounced a little different? In a deeper voice? No? Humbert. . . . Which is it now, first or second?

HUMBERT   (*getting more and more uneasy*) I wouldn't know.

CHARLOTTE   (*going to the phonograph*) I'll teach you the cha-cha-cha.
                (*returning to her armrest
                perch and coyly questioning*)
    Cha-cha-cha?

He rises from his low armchair, not because he wants to be taught but because the ripe lady might roll into his lap if he remains seated. The record clacks and croons. Charlotte demonstrates her ankles. Bored, helpless, Humbert, hands clasped on his fly, stands looking at her moving feet.

CHARLOTTE   It's as simple as that.
                    (*Darts to the phonograph*
                    to restart)
Now come here, Humbert.
                         (*smiling*)
That was *not* the surname.

Humbert surrenders. She leads him this way and that in a tactile drill. Releases him for a moment.

CHARLOTTE   Now do like this with your hands. More life. Fine. Now clasp me.

CUT TO:

Lawn Street in Front of No. 342
A station wagon with Mrs. Gray at the wheel, two or three boys and Lolita, stops at the lawn curb. Rigmarole of resonant good-byes. Car drives off. Lolita runs up the porch steps.

CUT TO:

Living Room
Charlotte pulsates and palpates Humbert's (stuffed) shoulder.

CHARLOTTE   In certain lights, when you frown like that, you remind me of somebody. A college boy I once danced with, a young blue-blooded Bostonian, my first glamour date.

The Door Chimes go into action.

CHARLOTTE   (*shutting off the record player*) Oh, darn it!

Humbert lets in Lolita.

LOLITA   (*casually*) Hullo, sweetheart.

She saunters into the living room.

CHARLOTTE   Well, you came earlier than I hoped—I mean, I did not hope you would be back so early.

LOLITA   You two seem to have been living it up here?

CHARLOTTE   How was your party?

LOLITA   Lousy.

CHARLOTTE   I thought Kenny looked cute.

LOLITA   I'm calling him Shorty from now on. I never realized he was so short. And dumb.

CHARLOTTE   Well, you've had your fling—and now to bed, my dear.

During this exchange, Humbert in abject adoration, gloats over the limp nymphet who has now filled a low chair with her foamy skirt and thin arms.

HUMBERT   You remind me of a sleepy flamingo.

LOLITA   Cut it out, Hum.

CHARLOTTE   Do you permit, Mr. Humbert, this rude child——

[62]

LOLITA   Oh, Mother, give us a break. May I take these
    cookies upstairs?

CHARLOTTE   Well, if you want to pamper your
    pimples——

LOLITA   I don't have pimples!

CHARLOTTE   Take anything you want but go.

LOLITA   All in good time.
                    (*Stretches.*)
    Did you talk to the famous author?

CHARLOTTE   Yes. Please go.

LOLITA   Rose is crazy about him. Okay, I go. Bye-bye.

Indolently she moves out of the room. At the bottom of the
stairs—as seen from the parlor—she stops, lingers, with her
fair arm stretched out on the rail and her cheek on her arm.
Meditates in this posture.

HUMBERT   What author did she mean?

CHARLOTTE   The author of *The Nymphet.* He's the
    nephew—will you *please* go upstairs, Lolita?

Lolita sighs, grimaces, and slowly comes into lazy motion.

HUMBERT   Thanks for this charming evening, Mrs.
    Haze.

CHARLOTTE   Thank *you,* Mr. Humbert. Oh, sit down.
    Let's have a nightcap.

HUMBERT   No, I think not. I think I'll go up to bed.

CHARLOTTE   It's quite early yet, you know.

HUMBERT   I know. But my neuralgia is about to strike.
. . . With heartburn, an old ally.

CUT TO:

Stairs and Upper Landing
The nymphet is still there, now sliding up dreamily, half-
reclining on the banisters. Humbert and she reach the upper
landing together.

HUMBERT   Good night, Lolita.

LOLITA   Huh?

HUMBERT   I said "good night, Lolita."

LOLITA   Night.

She totters to her room.

CUT TO:

Humbert's Study, a Couple of Days Later
Humbert in his room is tape-recording his lecture, "Baudelaire
and Poe." He plays back the last sentences:

HUMBERT'S VOICE   Before discussing Baudelaire's
methods of translating Poe, let me turn for a moment
to the romantic lines, let me turn to the romantic lines
in which the great American neurotic commemorates

his marriage to a thirteen-year-old girl, his beautiful
Annabel Lee.

(*The machine clicks and stops.*)

Now Lolita is heard bouncing a tennis ball. Humbert softly
opens his door and listens. She is in the hallway. Humming
to herself, Lolita walks upstairs plucking at the banisters and
quietly clowning. Bluejeans, shirt. Humbert is back in his
chair, Lolita is on the landing. With a good deal of shuffling
and scraping she comes into Humbert's room. She potters
around, fidgets, moves variously in the neighborhood of his
desk.

LOLITA   (*bending close to him*) What are you drawing?

HUMBERT   (*considering his drawing*) Is it you?

LOLITA   (*peering still more closely—she is somewhat
shortsighted*) Is it?

HUMBERT   Or perhaps it is more like a little girl I
knew when I was your age.

One of the drawers of the desk comes out by itself in a kind
of organic protractile movement, disclosing a photograph of
Humbert's first love in a Riviera setting: a sidewalk café
near a peopled *plage*.

LOLITA   Where's that?

HUMBERT   In a princedom by the sea. Monaco.

LOLITA   Oh, I know where that is.

HUMBERT   I'm sure you do. Many and many a year
    ago. Thirty, to be exact.

LOLITA   What was her name?

HUMBERT   Annabel—curiously enough.

LOLITA   Why curiously enough?

HUMBERT   Never mind. And this was me.

Same snapshot, same setting, but now in the photograph the
chair next to Annabel is occupied by young Humbert, a moody
lad. Morosely, he takes off his white cap as if acknowledging
recognition, and dons it again.
Actually it is the same actress as the one that plays Lolita but
wearing her hair differently, etc.

LOLITA   She doesn't look like me at all. Were you in
    love with her?

HUMBERT   Yes. Three months later she died. Here, on
    that beach, you see the angels envying her and me.

He clears his throat.

LOLITA   (now holding the photo) That's not angels.
    That's Garbo and Abraham Lincoln in terrycloth robes.

She laughs. A pause. As she bends her brown curls over the
picture, Humbert puts his arm around her in a miserable
imitation of blood relationship, and still studying the snapshot—which now shows young Humbert alone—Lolita slowly
sinks to a half-sitting position upon his knee.

    The erotic suspense is interrupted.

CHARLOTTE   (*shouting up from hallway*) Lolita! Will you come down, please?

LOLITA   (*without changing her position*) I'm busy! What d'you want?

CHARLOTTE   Will you come down at once?

At the Foot of the Stairs
Charlotte and Lolita.

CHARLOTTE   Now, firstly I want you to change. Put on a dress: I'm going to the Chatfields, and I want you to come too. Secondly: I simply forbid you to disturb Mr. Humbert. He's a writer and should not be disturbed. And if you make that grimace again, I think I'll slap you.

CUT TO:

Humbert Transcribing from Pad to Diary
speaks as he deciphers his jottings.

HUMBERT   (*in a low faltering voice*) The hag said she would slap Lolita, my Lolita. For thirty years I mourned Annabel, and watched nymphets playing in parks, and never once dared—. And now Annabel is dead, and Lolita is alive—my darling—"my darling—my life and my bride."

CUT TO:

Dinner with Charlotte

HUMBERT   And where is your daughter tonight?

CHARLOTTE   Oh, I left her at the Chatfields'—she's going to a movie with Phyllis. By the way, I have a glorious surprise for you.

HUMBERT   What surprise? One of your dramatic sweets?

CHARLOTTE   Wrong, Monsieur. Try again.

HUMBERT   A new light bulb.

CHARLOTTE   Nope.

HUMBERT   I give up.

CHARLOTTE   After tomorrow, Lolita is leaving for summer camp.

HUMBERT   (*trying to conceal his consternation*) Really? This is only June, you know.

CHARLOTTE   Exactly. I think of myself as a good average mother, but I confess I'm looking forward to ten full weeks of tranquillity. Another slice of beef? No?

HUMBERT   Toothache.

CHARLOTTE   Oh, you poor man! Let me have Dr. Quilty take care of you.

HUMBERT   No, no, don't bother. It will pass. How far is that camp?

CHARLOTTE   About two hundred miles. It was a stroke of genius on Mama's part. I arranged everything without telling little Lolita, who dislikes Phyllis for no reason at all. Sprang it upon her at the Chatfields', so she could not talk back. Ain't I clever? Little Lolita I hope will be mollified by the movie. I just could not have faced her tonight.

HUMBERT   Are you sure she will be happy at that camp?

CHARLOTTE   She'd better. She'll go riding there, which is much healthier than banging a tennis ball against the garage door. And camp will be much healthier than moping here, and pursuing shy scholarly gentlemen. Camp will teach Dolores to grow in many ways— health, knowledge, temper. And particularly in the sense of responsibility toward other people. Shall we take these candles with us and sit for a while on the piazza? Or do you want to go to bed and nurse that tooth?

HUMBERT   Tooth.

He slowly ascends the stairs. Charlotte calls after him.

CHARLOTTE   By the way—I told Lolita *you* had advised it. I thought your authority
               (*crystalline little laugh*)
would have more weight than mine.

Night. Humbert in His Room at the Window
Car stops at 342 Lawn Street.

CHARLOTTE   Oh, do come in for a moment, Mary. I forgot to check a few items on that list for the girls. Do come in.

MRS. CHATFIELD   Well, just for a minute.

CHARLOTTE   We excuse you, Dolores. Straight to bed like a good girl.

Humbert meets Lolita on the landing.

HUMBERT   (*attempting small talk*) How was the picture?

Without answering, Lolita marches toward her room.

HUMBERT   What's the matter, Lolita?

LOLITA   Nothing. Except that you are revolting.

HUMBERT   I did not do anything. It's a mistake. I swear.

LOLITA   (*haughtily*) I'm through with you. *Envoyez votre jeune fille au camp, Madame.* Double-crosser!

HUMBERT   I never said that! It's not even French! I'd do anything to have you stay here. I really would.

She slams the door.

CUT TO:

Humbert Dictates His "Baudelaire and Poe" lecture into the recorder.

HUMBERT   Other commentators, commentators of the Freudian school of thought. No. Commentators of the Freudian prison of thought. Hm. Commentators of the Freudian nursery-school of thought, have main-

tained that Edgar Poe married the child Virginia Clemm
merely to keep her mother near him. He—I quote—
had found in his mother-in-law Mrs. Clemm the mater-
nal image he had been seeking all his life. What piffle!
Listen now to the passion and despair breathing in the
letter he addresses to Virginia's mother on August 29,
1835, when he feared that his thirteen-year-old little
sweetheart would be taken away to be educated in another home. "I am blinded with tears while writing this
letter. . . . My last, my last, my only hold on life is
cruelly torn away. . . . My agony is more than I can
bear. . . . for love like mine can never be gotten over.
. . . It is useless to disguise the truth . . . that I shall
never behold her again. . . ."

CUT TO:

Humbert's Alarm Clock Rings
Sevent thirty. He hurries to the window.

SHOT FROM ABOVE

The maid helps to put a bag into the car. Lolita is leaving for
camp.

CHARLOTTE   Hurry up, Lolita.

Lolita is now half in and about to pull the car door to, but
suddenly she looks up—and scurries back into the house.

CHARLOTTE   (*furiously*) Dolores, get back into the car
     immediately!

She does not heed her mother's shout. She runs upstairs. She
wears her Sunday frock—gay cotton, with ample skirt and

fitting bodice. Humbert has come out on the landing. She stomps upstairs and next moment is in his arms. Hers is a perfectly innocent impulse, an affectionate bright farewell. As she rises on tiptoe to kiss him, he evades her approaching lips and imprints a poetical kiss on her brow.

CHARLOTTE   (*Blows the horn.*)

Lolita flies downstairs, gestures up to him in a ballerina-like movement of separation, and is gone.

The blond leg is drawn in, the car door slams, is reslammed as the car gathers momentum to the sound of the collie's *Bark.*

CUT TO:

Silence—except for the birds outside and the young Negro maid in the kitchen. The telephone *rings.*

MAID   No, there's no Miss Lee here. You must have got the wrong number. You're welcome.

Humbert has remained standing on the landing between his open door and the open door of Lolita's room opposite.

He surveys her deserted room. Abandoned clothes lie on the rumpled bed. A pair of white shoes with roller skates on the floor. He rolls one on his palm.

There is a full-page advertisement (back cover of magazine) tacked onto the wall: a distinguished playwright solemnly smoking ("I can write without a pen, but not without a Drome"). After a moment's brooding, Humbert goes to his room and incontinently starts to pack. Knock on his door.

The maid Louise knocks on Humbert's door. He opens. She hands him a letter.

LOUISE   Mrs. Haze asked me to give you this, Mr. Humbert.

Humbert inspects envelope.

LOUISE   I'll be doing the girl's room now. And when I've done I'd like to do yours. And then I'll go.

Humbert, puckering brow at envelope, walks slowly back to his desk.

The neat handwriting of the address turns momentarily into a schoolgirl's scribble, then reverts to the ladylike hand. He opens the letter.

Humbert, in a classical pattern of comments, ironical asides, and well-mouthed readings, scans the letter. In one SHOT, he is dressed as a gowned professor, in another as a routine Hamlet, in a third, as a dilapidated Poe. He also appears as himself.

HUMBERT   "This is a confession, this is an avowal of love." No signature—what, no signature? Ah, here it is. Good God! "I have loved you from the moment I saw you. I am a lonely woman and you are the love of my love." Of "my life," I suppose.

As in a pimp's sample album, Charlotte appears in various unattractive attitudes and positions.

HUMBERT   "Now, my dearest, *mon cher, cher Monsieur,*" that's a new one: she thinks it's a term of endearment. "Now, you have read this, now you know. So will you please, *at once,* pack and leave: this is a land-lady's order. I shall be back by dinner time if I do eighty both ways and don't have an accident. But what would it matter?" I beg your pardon: it matters a lot *one* way. "You see, *chéri,*" ah, French improving, "*if* you decided to stay, if I found you there when I got home, it would mean only one thing—that you want me as much as I do you—as a lifelong mate; and that you are ready to link up your life with mine forever and be a father to my little girl." My dear Mrs. Haze, or rather Mrs. Clemm, I am passionately devoted to your daughter.

Pensively, with a dawning smile, Humbert starts to take out, one by one, slowly, then faster, the articles he had already packed. Then he goes into an awkward and grotesque jig (in striking contrast to his usual mournful and dignified demeanor). Dancing, he descends the stairs.

CUT TO:

Humbert
making a long-distance call.

HUMBERT   Is this Camp Q on Lake Climax?
                    (*Listens.*)
    Is Mrs. Haze still there? She brought her daughter to-day.
                    (*Listens.*)
    Oh, I see. Could I speak to Dolores Haze, Lolita?

He listens, waits.

LOLITA   Hullo?

[74]

Now both parties are visible in a montage arrangement, with the camp's various activities illustrated at the corners as in a publicity folder.

HUMBERT   I have news for you.

LOLITA   Hullo?

HUMBERT   This is Humbert. I have news for you.

She is holding a big pup.

LOLITA   Oh, how are you? I have a friend here who wants to say hullo.

The pup licks the receiver.

HUMBERT   Listen, Lolita. I'm going to marry your mother. I'm going to propose to her as soon as she's back.

LOLITA   Gee, that's swell. Look, I've got to get rid of this beast, he's too heavy. One sec. There.

HUMBERT   Will you come to the wedding?

LOLITA   What? I can't hear too well.

HUMBERT   Will you come to the wedding?

LOLITA   I'm not sure. No, I guess, I have to stay here. It's a *fabulous* place! There's a water-sports competition scheduled. And I'm learning to ride. And my tentmate is the Ramsdale junior swimming champion. And——

The Honeymooners
A month has elapsed. Kitchen at 342 Lawn Street.

Charlotte (radiant and demure, in tight velvet pants and bed slippers) prepares breakfast for two in the cute breakfast nook of the chrome-and-plastic kitchen. Shadows of sun and leaves play on the white refrigerator. Humbert, in the wake of his yawn, enters (dressing gown, rumpled hair).

Charlotte makes him a jocular Oriental bow. His face twitching with neuralgia, he glances at the scrambled eggs and starts clawing at a cupboard.

CHARLOTTE   What are you looking for?

HUMBERT   Pepper.

A tennis ball jumps out of the cupboard.

HUMBERT   I wonder if she can play tennis at that damned camp.

CHARLOTTE   I could not care less. Look what the *Ramsdale Journal* has to say about us. Here. Society Column.

Humbert glances at paper.

CHARLOTTE   Isn't that something? Look at your elegant bride. "Mr. Edgar H. Humbert, writer and explorer, weds the former——" I never knew you were Edgar.

HUMBERT   Oh, I called up a reporter and thought I'd inject a little glamour.

He yawns again.

CHARLOTTE   And what have you explored?

HUMBERT   Madame should not ask vulgar questions.

CHARLOTTE   (*very arch*) And Monsieur has certainly a grand sense of humor.

Charlotte Is Showing Bored Humbert
some of her treasures. A lamplit evening at the Humbert residence.

HUMBERT   (*suddenly interested*) Hey, a gun.

He examines a small automatic.

CHARLOTTE   It belonged to Mr. Haze.

HUMBERT   Hm. And then suddenly it went off.

CHARLOTTE   It's not loaded.

HUMBERT   That's what they all say: "I did not know it was loaded."

CHARLOTTE   Who—they?

HUMBERT   Boy shoots girl, banker shoots bitch, rapist shoots therapist.

CHARLOTTE   I told you many times that I appreciated your humor, but now and then it is misplaced. This is a sacred weapon, a tragic treasure. Mr. Haze acquired it when he thought he had cancer. He wanted to spare me the sight of his sufferings. Happily, or unhappily, he was hospitalized before he could use it. And this is me just before I married him.

In the snapshot Charlotte at twenty-five resembles her daughter more than she does now. Humbert is moved.

HUMBERT   I like this one tremendously. May I have it?

CHARLOTTE   Oh, my dear, of course! Everything is yours. Wait, let me inscribe it.

Charlotte writes on the photo: For my *chéri* Humbert from his Charlotte. April 1946 [if it is now 1960.]

CUT TO:

Humbert and Wife in Car
He is driving her to the lake.

HUMBERT   What's that palazzo? A brothel?

CHARLOTTE   That's Jerome McFate's house. He's manager of our bank, if you please.

HUMBERT   What a name for a banker.

They leave the car at the edge of the pine forest and walk through it to the lake. They are sandaled and robed.

CHARLOTTE   Do you know, Hum, I have one most ambitious dream. I should love to get hold of a real French servant like that German girl the Talbots had, and have her live in the house.

[78]

HUMBERT   No room.

CHARLOTTE   Come.
          (*with a quizzical smile*)
Surely, *chéri*, you underestimate the possibilities of the
Humbert home. We would put her in Lo's room. I intended to make a guest room of that hole anyway. It's
the coldest and meanest in the whole house.

HUMBERT   And where, pray, will you put your daughter
when you get your guest or your maid?

CHARLOTTE   (*softly exhaling and raising one eye-
brow*) Ah! Little Lo, I'm afraid, does not enter the picture at all, at all. Little Lo goes straight from camp to a
good boarding school with strict discipline. I have it all
mapped out, you need not worry.

The Brilliant Lake
There is a moored raft some forty yards off the lake shore.
Humbert and Charlotte on the sandy strip. He, sitting, hands
clasping knees, in a dreadful frame of mind; she, serenely and
luxuriously reclining.

HUMBERT   The sand is filthy. Some oaf has been walking his filthy dog. And there's a chewing-gum wrapper.

CHARLOTTE   Oh, those are just leftovers from Sunday.
There's not a soul anywhere. It's not at all like the east
end of the lake where they built the casino.

HUMBERT   One would think there would be some
decrepit cripple with a piked stick cleaning up on
Mondays.

CHARLOTTE   No, I don't think so. In fact, even on weekends there is hardly anybody bathing at this end. This is the restricted part. We are alone, sweetheart, you and me. And we'll remain so forever. Just you and me. A red cent for your thoughts.

HUMBERT   I was wondering if you could make it to that raft, or whatever it is. I loathe this dirty gray sand. Out there we could sunbathe in the
                    (*wrinkling his nose*)
nude, as you genteel Americans say.

CHARLOTTE   I doubt it. This American's back is burnt as it is. Besides, I couldn't swim that far.

HUMBERT   Nonsense. Your merman will be at your side.

CHARLOTTE   How deep would you say it is?

HUMBERT   Twice your height. Two wives.

CHARLOTTE   I'm sure to panic and drown.

HUMBERT   All right, all right. If you don't want to swim, let's go home. This place bores me stiff.

CHARLOTTE   Well, I can always try.

DISSOLVE:

Humbert and Charlotte
reach the raft.

CHARLOTTE   Ah! I thought I would never make it.

[80]

HUMBERT   Yes, but there's still the return voyage.

An airplane passes overhead.

CHARLOTTE   That's a private plane, isn't it?

HUMBERT   I've no idea. That guardian angel has been
    circling above the lake during our entire swim. I think
    he's leaving now.

A butterfly passes in shorebound flight.

CHARLOTTE   Can butterflies swim?

HUMBERT   (*indistinct answer*)

CHARLOTTE   Shall I risk taking off my bra?

HUMBERT   I don't give a damn.

CHARLOTTE   Will you give a damn if I kiss you?

He grunts. Pause.

DISSOLVE TO:

Another Angle

CHARLOTTE   Not a cloud, not a soul, not a sound.

HUMBERT   Let's swim back.

CHARLOTTE   What—already? We haven't been here
    ten minutes.

HUMBERT   Come on, let's go in.

CHARLOTTE   Please, Humbert, stop pushing me.

HUMBERT   I'll roll you in the water.

CHARLOTTE   You'll do nothing of the sort. We are going to stay here till the Farlows come.

HUMBERT   They won't be here for another hour.

CHARLOTTE   Relax and enjoy yourself. Tell me about your first wife.

HUMBERT   To hell with her.

CHARLOTTE   You are very rude, sweetheart.

HUMBERT   I'm very bored. Look here. The Farlows will retrieve you. I'm going home. *Au revoir.*

He dives and swims away.

CHARLOTTE   Oh, please. Wait! I'm coming too. Oh, wait!

He swims on without turning his head. Awkwardly, she lowers herself into the water. He is now nearing the shore. She starts swimming and almost immediately is seized with a cramp.

A neat little diagram shows the relative positions of a drowning person (one arm sticking out of the water), a stationary raft, and the shoreline at equal distance from the sufferer.

For a few seconds, Humbert floats motionless in a vertical position, his chin just above the surface, his eyes fixed on floundering Charlotte. There should be something reptilian and spine-chilling in his expectant stare. Then, as she gasps, and sinks, and splashes, and screams, he dashes toward her, reaching her in a few strokes.

He helps her out onto the beach.

CHARLOTTE   (*still panting*) You know—you know —for one moment—I thought you—would not come to save me—your eyes—you looked at me with dreadful, dreadful eyes——

He soothes her in a humid embrace.

CUT TO:

Car
They are driving home.

CHARLOTTE   You know, it's so funny. A drowning person is said to recollect his entire life but all I re-membered was last night's dream. You were offering me some pill or potion, and a voice said: Careful, Isolda, that's poison.

HUMBERT   Rather pointless—what?

The car pulls up at 342 Lawn Street. They get out.

HUMBERT   Here, take this towel. Oh, blast it! I forgot my sunglasses on that bloody beach.

CHARLOTTE   Were they very expensive?

[83]

HUMBERT   (*still searching*) I loved them. They made
    a kind of taupe twilight. I bought them in St.-Topaz,
    never mislaid them before.

CHARLOTTE   Why don't you drive back to the lake
    and find them? Kiss?
                    (*Humbert obliges.*)
    Meantime I'll tidy up——

CUT TO:

The "Semi-Studio"
Taking advantage of Humbert's absence, Charlotte lovingly
cleans his den. A small key drops out of a jacket. She considers it for a moment with amused perplexity; then tries it in
the lock of a certain small drawer. The treasure turns out to
be a little black book, Humbert's dark diary. She flips it open.
Her daughter's name leers at her from every page. But the
microscopic script is hard to decipher. She snatches up a mag-
nifying glass. In its bland circle Humbert's jottings leap into
formidable life:
"*... but her grotesque mother butted in .... Friday: She is a
bitch, that Haze woman. She is sending my darling away. Alas,
Lolita! Farewell, my love! If the old cat expects me to stay
on, she is——*"

CUT TO:

Humbert
opening the door of his living room. Charlotte, with her back
to him, is writing at the desk in the far corner.

HUMBERT   I'm back. Couldn't find them.

[84]

Charlotte does not answer but her writing hand stops. She turns slowly toward him revealing a face disfigured by grief and wrath.

CHARLOTTE   "The Haze woman," "the old cat," "the obnoxious mama," "the—the old stupid Haze," is no longer your dupe.

HUMBERT   But what——

CHARLOTTE   You're a monster, you're a detestable, abominable, criminal fraud! If you come near me, I'll scream out the window.

HUMBERT   But really——

CHARLOTTE   I'm leaving today. This is all yours. Only you'll never, never see that miserable brat again.

HUMBERT   I can explain everything.

CHARLOTTE   Get out of here. Oh, I can see it all now. You tried to drown me, you would have shot me or poisoned me next. You disgusting satyr. I'm applying for a job in Parkington and you'll never see me again.

Furiously, she rummages for the stamps she needs. The convex block of them has fallen on the carpet. Tears off one, two. Fast and furious. Thumps on envelope.

CUT TO:

Humbert
goes swiftly upstairs to his study. There he contemplates the open and empty drawer. He crosses over to the bedroom and

starts looking for his diary, which he suspects she has hidden. After some rapid ransacking, he finds it under her pillow. He walks downstairs again.

CUT TO:

Kitchen
He opens the refrigerator. Its roar, as well as the crepitation of the ice cubes in their cells under warm water, the noisy faucet, the fussing with the whiskey and soda, the banging of cupboard doors, and Humbert's own mutter, drown the *Sounds* from the street (such as the hideous screech of desperate brakes).

HUMBERT   (*muttering*) Tell her ... Misunderstood ... Civilized people . . . Brought you a drink . . . Don't be ridiculous . . . Fragments of novel . . . Provisional names . . . The notes you found were fragments of a novel. . . .

He has now prepared his defense. Carrying the two glasses he leaves the kitchen.

CUT TO:

Hallway-Door of Living Room Slightly Ajar
As Humbert approaches the *Telephone Rings* on table near door. He places the glasses on the table and lifts the receiver.

VOICE   This is Lesley Tompson, the gardener next door. Your wife, sir, has been run over and you'd better come quick.

HUMBERT   Nonsense. My wife is here—
                  (*Pushes the door open.*)
           man saying you've been killed, Charlotte. . . .

The room is empty. He turns back, the front door is not shut, the receiver is still throbbing on the table. He rushes out. "The far side of our steep little street presented a peculiar sight. A big black limousine had climbed Miss Opposite's sloping lawn at an angle from the sidewalk."

The picture now is a still. Humbert surveys the scene: The body on the sidewalk, the old gentleman resting on the grass near the car, various people attracted by the accident, the unfortunate driver, two policemen, and the cheerful collie walking from group to group.

A photographer from the Traffic Division is taking a picture.

In a projection room it is shown to a bunch of policemen by an instructor with a pointer:

THE INSTRUCTOR   Now, this is the picture of a real accident. To the ordinary spectator who has just arrived on the scene the situation may seem very, very unusual: it is not so, really. The lap robe there, on the sidewalk, covers a dead woman. The elderly person here on the grass is not dead but comfortably recovering from a mild heart attack. His nephew, the fat fellow talking to the police officers, was driving him to a birthday party when they ran over this woman. This is their car up on the slope of the lawn where it came to rest after leaving the road. It was moving down the street like so.

A diagram now appears with arrows and dotted lines.

INSTRUCTOR   The driver was trying to avoid the dog. The woman was crossing here. She was in a great hurry to mail a letter but never made it to the mailbox.
        (*still picture again*)

That man there who stands looking stunned is her husband.

The still comes to life. A little girl picks up the letter which Charlotte was about to post and hands it to Humbert. Old Mr. Jung is sobbing uncontrollably. The ambulance arrives. The Farlows lead Humbert away.

Act Two

The Office of Camp Q, a Stucco Cottage — early afternoon
The camp mistress hangs up and calls a camp counselor.

CAMP MISTRESS   (*to counselor*) Mr. Humbert has
just telephoned. Lolita's mother has been killed in a
street accident.

COUNSELLOR   Oh, my gosh.

CAMP MISTRESS   He's on the way here to fetch her.
He asked me to tell her that her mother is sick. Find
the girl, please, and have her get ready to leave. By the
way, where's that lazy son of mine—make him move the
garbage cans to the back of the shed.

CUT TO:

The Search for Lolita
Her name is cried out in different voices and keys at various
points. We pass in review the awfully quaint cabins and tents
in a pine grove. The camera looks behind trees and bushes.
Two shadows hastily unclip in the undergrowth. Distant cries
swell and recede.

Lolita! Lolita!

CUT TO:

Dirt Road
leading to cabins and tents. Humbert drives up. Charlie, the camp mistress's fourteen-year-old-son, is rolling an empty garbage can across the road.

HUMBERT (*out of car window, pointing questioningly*)
Is that the office?

Charlie mutely directs him with a jerk of his thumb.

CUT TO:

Camp Office—Humbert and the Camp Mistress

CAMP MISTRESS (*computing the bill and not raising her eyes from her writing*) What a terrible accident! When is the funeral?

HUMBERT Oh, that was yesterday. It was decided not to have the child attend. Spare her the shock.

He settles the bill.

CAMP MISTRESS Thank you. The poor kid. Here's your receipt.

Lolita arrives, dragging and bumping her valise.

LOLITA Hi.

He lets his hand rest on her head and takes up her bag. She wears her brightest gingham and saddle oxfords.

As Humbert and she walk toward the car, Lolita waves to Charlie.

LOLITA   Good-bye, Charlie boy!

Moodily, not without some regret, he follows her with his pale, fair-lashed eyes.

CUT TO:

The Hot Car (*inside*)
She settles down beside Humbert, slaps a prompt fly on her lovely knee; then, her mouth working violently on chewing gum, she rapidly cranks down the window. The car speeds through the striped and speckled forest.

LOLITA   (*dutifully*) How's mother?

HUMBERT   It's something abdominal.

LOLITA   Abominable?

HUMBERT   No, abdominal. A stomach ailment. She's been moved to a hospital in the country. Not far from Lepingsville.

LOLITA   Are we going to, what you called it—Lepersville?

HUMBERT   Lepingsville. Yes, I expect we'll have to hang around a bit while she gets better or at least a little better. And then we'll go to the mountains. Is that a peachy idea?

LOLITA   Uh-huh. How far is it to her hospital?

[91]

HUMBERT   Oh, two hundred miles. Did you have a marvelous time at the camp?

LOLITA   Uh-huh.

HUMBERT   Sorry to leave?

LOLITA   Un-un.

HUMBERT   Talk, Lolita, don't grunt. Tell me something.

LOLITA   What thing, *Dad?*

HUMBERT   Any old thing.

LOLITA   Okay if I call you that?

HUMBERT   Quite.

LOLITA   It's a sketch, you know——

HUMBERT   A what?

LOLITA   A scream: you falling for my mummy.

HUMBERT   There are also such things as mutual respect and spiritual happiness.

LOLITA   Sure, sure.

(The lull in the dialogue is filled in with some landscapes).

HUMBERT   Look at all those cows on the hillside.

LOLITA   I'll vomit if I see another cow.

HUMBERT   You know I missed you terribly, Lolita Lo. Really and truly.

LOLITA   I didn't. Fact I've been revoltingly unfaithful to you, but it doesn't matter a bit because you've stopped caring for me, anyway. You drive much faster than my mummy, mister.

He slows down from 70 to 50 as seen on speedometer.

HUMBERT   Why do you think I've stopped caring for you?

LOLITA   Well, you haven't kissed me yet, have you?

Humbert wobbles into the roadside weeds and stops. She cuddles up to him. A highway patrol car draws up alongside.

POLICEMAN   Having trouble?

HUMBERT   No, no. I just wanted to look at the map.

LOLITA   (*eagerly leaning across H.H. and speaking with unusual urbanity*) I'm afraid we have parked where we shouldn't but there was some question of taking a short cut, and we thought——

POLICEMAN   Well, if you want to stop there's a picnic area three hundred yards from here.

LOLITA   Oh, thank you.

The beetle-browed trooper gives the little colleen his toothiest smile and glides away. Lolita presses a fluttering hand to her breastbone.

LOLITA   The fruithead! He should have nabbed you.

HUMBERT   Why me, for heaven's sake?

LOLITA   Because the speed limit in this bum state is
             fifty. No, don't slow down. He's gone now.

HUMBERT   We have still quite a stretch, so be a good
             girl.

LOLITA   That light was red. I've never seen such driving.

They roll silently through a silent townlet.

HUMBERT   You said you'd been—I don't know—
             naughty? Don't you want to tell me about that?

LOLITA   Are you easily shocked?

HUMBERT   No. What did you do?

LOLITA   Well, I joined in all the activities that were
             offered.

HUMBERT   *Ensuite?*

LOLITA   Ansooit, I was taught to live happily and richly
             with others and to develop a wholesome personality.
             Be a cake, actually.

HUMBERT   Yes, I saw that in the camp booklet.

LOLITA   We loved the sings around the fire.

HUMBERT   Anything else?

[94]

LOLITA   (*rhapsodically*) The Girl Scout's motto is also mine. My duty is to be useful to animals. I obey orders. I am cheerful. And I am absolutely filthy in thought, word, and deed.

HUMBERT   Is that all, young wit?

LOLITA   We baked in a reflector oven. Isn't that terrific? Oh, gee! We made shadowgraphs. We identified the three birds teacher knew. What fun!

HUMBERT   *C'est bien tout?*

LOLITA   *C'est.* Except one little thing that I may tell you later in the dark.

CUT TO:

The Road
A sign by the side of the road says 8 MILES TO ENCHANTED HUNTERS. Further, another sign BRICELAND, ELEV. 759 FEET. Finally a sign at a crossing 3 MILES TO ENCHANTED HUNTERS—YE UNFORGETTABLE INN.

LOLITA   Oh, let's stop at the unforgettable!

HUMBERT   I've reserved rooms in a tourist home at Lepingsville, but——

LOLITA   Oh, please. Let's go to the Enchanted. It's a famous romantic place. We'll make people think you've eloped with me. Please!

. . . And there it was, marvelously and inexorably there, at the top of a graded curve under spectral trees, at the top of a graveled drive—the pale palace of The Enchanted Hunters.

LOLITA   (*getting out of the car*) Wow! Looks swank.

Old Tom, a hunchbacked and hoary Negro, takes out the bags.

It is a large old heavily quaint family hotel with a pillared porch. Humbert and Lolita enter the ornate lounge. Two conventions, a medical one on the ebb and a floral one on the flow, throng the reception rooms.

Lolita sinks down on her haunches to caress a cocker spaniel sprawling and melting under her hand.

HUMBERT   (*At the reception desk* talks to Mr. Potts, the clerk,
                    indistinctly)
I want a room for the night.

POTTS   Excuse me, sir?

HUMBERT   I want two rooms or one room with two beds.

POTTS   I'm not sure we can accommodate you. We have the overflow of a convention of doctors from another hotel and we also have a reunion of rose growers just budding. Is it for you and your little girl?

He looks kindly at Lolita.

HUMBERT   Her mother is ill. We are very tired.

POTTS   Mr. Swoon!

Swoon, another clerk, appears.

POTTS   What about Dr. Love, has he called?

SWOON   He has canceled his reservation.

POTTS   And what about the Bliss family?

SWOON   They are supposed to check out tonight.

POTTS   (*to Humbert*) Well, I could give you 342. But it has one bed.

HUMBERT   Could you put in a cot perhaps?

POTTS   We have none available at the moment but the situation may improve later.

HUMBERT   Well, I'll register.

POTTS   It's really quite a large
                    (*opens the book*)
bed. The other night we had three doctors sleeping in it, and the middle one was a pretty broad
                    (*offers the desk pen to Humbert
                    whose own pen has stalled*)
gentleman.

Third-Floor Corridor
Uncle Tom, with bags and key, opens the door for Humbert and Lolita. There is some fussing with the key.

LOLITA   Oh, look! It's the same number as our house. 342.

HUMBERT   Funny coincidence.

LOLITA   Yes. Very funny. You know
                    (*laughing*)
last night I dreamt mother got drowned in Ramsdale
Lake.

HUMBERT   Oh.

. CUT TO:

Room

There's a double bed, a mirror, a double bed in the mirror, a
closet door with mirror, a bathroom door ditto, a blue-
dark window, a reflected bed there, the same in the closet
mirror, two chairs, a glass-topped table, two bed tables, a
double bed: a big panel bed, to be exact, with a Tuscan rose
chenille spread, and two frilled, pink-shaded nightlamps,
left and right.

Humbert tips old Tom one dollar, calls him back, and
adds another. Exit Tom, gratefully grinning.

LOLITA   (*her features working*)
You mean we are *both* going to sleep *here?*

HUMBERT   I've asked them to give me a separate room
     or at least to put in a cot—for you or me, as you wish.

LOLITA   You are crazy.

HUMBERT   Why, my darling?

LOLITA   Because, my dahrling, when dahrling Mother
     finds out, she'll divorce you and strangle me.

She stands slitting her eyes at herself contentedly in the
closet door mirror. Humbert has sat down on the edge of a

low chair, nervously rubbing his hands and leaning toward her pleased reflection.

HUMBERT   Now look here, Lo. Let's settle this once for all. I'm your stepfather. In your mother's absence I'm responsible for your welfare. We shall be a lot together. And since we are not rich, we won't be able
                    (*Gets up and hangs up his*
                    raincoat, which however
                    slips off the hanger.)
    to have *always* two rooms.

LOLITA   Okay. I want my comb.

Humbert tries to embrace her—casually, a bit of controlled tenderness before dinner.

LOLITA   Look, let's cut out the kissing game and get something to eat.

He opens the suitcase with the articles he bought for her.

HUMBERT   By the way—here are some frocks and things I got for you at Parkington.

"Oh, what a dreamy pet! She walked up to the open suitcase as if stalking it from afar, at a kind of slow-motion walk, peering at that distant treasure box on the luggage support." She raises by the armlets a garment, pulls out the slow snake of a brilliant belt, tries it on. "Then she crept into my waiting arms, radiant, relaxed, caressing me with her tender, mysterious, impure, indifferent twilight eyes—for all the world like the cheapest of cheap cuties. For that is what nymphets imitate—while we moan and die." Their kiss is interrupted by a knock on the door. Old Tom enters with a vase of magnificent roses.

HUMBERT   Well! Where do these come from?

TOM   *I* don't know.

HUMBERT   What do you mean—you don't know? Is it the management?

TOM   I don't know. I was given them at the flower counter. For Mister—
               (*Glances at the card.*)
    Mister Homberg and his little girl.

Exit Uncle Tom, with a quarter.

HUMBERT (*shrugging it off*) Seems that flower show had a surplus of roses. I detest flowers. And I also detest when my name is misspelt.

LOLITA   Oh, but they are gorgeous!

(The point is, of course, that the bouquet is from an old admirer of little Dolores, Clare Quilty, whom we shall glimpse presently.)

CUT TO:

Dining Room at the Enchanted Hunters
A pretentious mural depicts enchanted hunters in various postures and states of enchantment amid a medley of animals, dryads, cypresses, and porticoes.

LOLITA (*considering the mural*) What does it *mean*?

HUMBERT   Oh, mythological scenes, modernized. Bad art, anyway.

LOLITA   What's bad art?

HUMBERT   The work of a mediocre derivative artist. Look at that crummy unicorn. Or is it a centaur?

LOLITA   He's not crummy. He's wonderful.

Waitress brings food.

CUT TO:

End of Meal
Humbert produces a vial of sleeping pills, removes the stopper and tips the container into his palm. He claps a hand to his mouth and feigns swallowing.

LOLITA   Purple pills—what are they?

HUMBERT   Vitamin P. Purple seas and plums, and plumes of paradise birds. And peat bog orchids. And Priap's orchard.

LOLITA   And double talk. Gimme one quick!

HUMBERT   Here.

Out of his fist the pill he had palmed is slipped into her gay cupped little hand.

LOLITA   (*swallowing*) I bet it's a love philter.

HUMBERT   Good gracious! What do you know about philters?

LOLITA   Just a movie I saw. *Stan and Izzie*. With Mark King. Oh, look who's here.

A man in a loud sports jacket comes into the dining room and walks to a distant table. It is Quilty. He recognizes Mrs. Haze's fascinating little girl but except for a glance of amused appraisal does not pay any attention to Humbert and her.

LOLITA   Doesn't he look exactly, but exactly, like Quilty?

HUMBERT   (*frightened*) What? Our fat dentist is here?

Lolita arrests the mouthful of water she has just taken and sets down her dancing glass.

LOLITA   (*with a splutter of mirth*) 'Course not. I meant the writer fellow in the *Drome* ad.

HUMBERT   O Fame, O Femina.

WAITRESS   What would you like for dessert? We have ice cream—raspberry, chocolate, vanilla and let me see——

LOLITA   Chocolate and raspberry for me.

HUMBERT   And for me just a cup of coffee. And the check, please.

Lolita shakes her curls trying to dismiss somnolence.

HUMBERT   When did they make you get up at camp?

LOLITA   Half past
                    (*She stifles a big yawn.*)
        six.
                    (*yawn in full swell, shiver
                    of all her frame*)
        Half past six.
                    (*throat fills up
                    again*)
        I went canoeing this morning, and after that——

WAITRESS   We did not have the raspberry after all.

DISSOLVE TO:

The Elevator
Enter Humbert and Lolita; three rose-growing ladies each
looking like a rock garden; two old men; and the elevator
girl. Humbert and Lolita face each other closely, then still
more closely as others crowd in. The two men get out. Lolita
somnolent and sly, pressed against Humbert, raises her eyes
to him and laughs softly.

HUMBERT   What's the matter?

LOLITA   Nothing.

The three smiling matrons get out. There is now sufficient
room for H. and L. to stand apart.

OPERATOR   Watch your step, please.

CUT TO:

Corridor to Room 342

LOLITA   You ought to carry me as they do in cartoons. Oh, I'm so sleepy. Guess I'll have to tell you how naughty Charlie and me have been.

CUT TO:

Room 342

LOLITA   This bed sleeps two.

HUMBERT   It's yours.

LOLITA   Where is *your* room?

Yawning, she sits on the edge of the bed, removes her shoes and peels off one sock.

HUMBERT   I don't know yet. Brush your teeth or whatever you're supposed to do and go to bed.
          (*Opens her overnight case.*)
     Here are your things. I want you to be asleep when I come back. I'm going downstairs. Please, Lolita. No, that's the closet. The bathroom is there.

LOLITA   Mirror, mirror——

She laughs drowsily and exits.

CUT TO:

Humbert Leaves the Room and Walks Downstairs
As he nears the lobby and turns a corner he is brushed by the shoulder of a lurching, elated man (Quilty).

Humbert asks a bellboy the way to the bar.

BELLBOY   There is no bar.

HUMBERT   I wonder where that lush got his liquor.

BELLBOY   Oh, that's Mr. Quilty, sir. And he would not want to be bothered. He comes here to write.

HUMBERT   I see. Can you direct me to the washroom.

BELLBOY   To your left and down.

CUT TO:

Humbert
emerging from the lavatory. A hearty old party, Dr. Braddock, on the way in, greets him.

DR. BRADDOCK   Well, how did you like Dr. Boyd's speech? Oh, I'm sorry. I mistook you for Jack Bliss.

Humbert passes a group of women who are bound for the Rose Room. He consults his watch. He lingers for a moment in the lobby. Mr. Potts, noticing him but by him unnoticed, lifts a finger, then calls old Tom and gives him an order. Humbert consults his watch again and continues his restless loitering. He strolls out onto the dimly lit pillared porch. To one side in the darkness two or more people are sitting. We distinguish vaguely a very old man, and beyond him another person's shoulder. It is from these shadows that a voice (Quilty's) comes. It is preceded by the rasp of a screwing off, then a discrete gurgle, then the final note of a placid screwing on.

QUILTY'S VOICE   Where the devil did you get her?

HUMBERT   I beg your pardon?

QUILTY'S VOICE   I said: the weather is getting better.

HUMBERT   Seems so.

QUILTY'S VOICE   Who's the lassie?

HUMBERT   My daughter.

QUILTY'S VOICE   You lie—she's not.

HUMBERT   I beg your pardon?

QUILTY'S VOICE   I said: July was hot. Where's her mother?

HUMBERT   Dead.

QUILTY'S VOICE   I see. Sorry. By the way, why don't you two lunch with me tomorrow. That dreadful crowd will be gone by then.

HUMBERT   We'll be gone, too. Good night.

QUILTY'S VOICE   Sorry. I'm pretty drunk. Good night. That child of yours needs a lot of sleep. Sleep is a rose, as the Persians say. Smoke?

HUMBERT   Not now.

CUT TO:

Humbert Leaves the Porch
Sufficient time has elapsed. He tries not to display any hurry. As he makes his way through a constellation of fixed people in

[106]

one corner of the lobby near the dining room, there comes a blinding flash, as beaming Dr. Braddock and some matrons are photographed.

DR. BRADDOCK   (*pointing to part of the mural which continues around the corner*) And here the theme changes. The hunter thinks he has hypnotized the little nymph but it is she who puts him into a trance.

Humbert Walks up the Stairs
and turns in to the corridor. The door key with its large unwieldly hangpiece of polished wood is dangling from his hand. He takes off his coat. He stands for a moment immobile before door 342. It is a moment of wholesome hesitation. From the service elevator old Tom, the gray-haired Negro, hobbles out trundling a folded cot. Humbert turns guiltily.

TOM   342. I've brought you the cot, sir.

HUMBERT   Oh? Yes, yes, of course. But I'm afraid she is fast asleep. She has had a strenuous day.

TOM   That's quite all right. We'll put it in gently.

Humbert opens the door. Soft and slow, the rhythm of the young sleeper's respiration is kept ajar for ten seconds.

HUMBERT   Please, very quietly. I don't want the child to be disturbed.

Crablike, crippled old Tom unfolds the cot alongside the bed and shuffles out. Once out, he performs very slowly the act of closing a creaky door but at the last moment (the poor devil being somewhat spastic) he bangs it shut. Lolita does not wake up. Humbert (now in pajamas) tests and retests the security of her drugged sleep. He turns on the radio. She does not stir. A fist pounds on the wall. He shuts off the radio and touches her shoulder. Still she sleeps. That drug certainly works. He is about to take advantage of this safe sleep, but as the moon reaches her face, its innocent helpless fragile infantine beauty arrests him. He slinks back to his cot.

CUT TO:

Humbert Lying on His Cot supine, traversed by pale strips of moonlight coming through the slits in the blinds. Clouds engulf the moon.

"There is nothing louder than an American hotel; and, mind you, this was supposed to be a quiet, cozy, old-fashioned, homey place—'gracious living' and all that stuff. The clatter of the elevator's gate—some twenty yards northeast of my head but as clearly perceived as if it were inside my left temple—alternated with the banging and booming of the machine's various evolutions and lasted well beyond midnight. Every now and then, immediately east of my left ear, the corridor would brim with cheerful, resonant, and inept exclamations ending in a volley of good nights. When *that* stopped, a toilet immediately north of my cerebellum took over. It was a manly, energetic, deep-throated toilet, and it was used many times. Its gurgle and gush and long afterflow shook the wall behind me. Then someone in a southern direction was extravagantly sick, almost coughing out his life with his liquor, and his toilet descended like a veritable Niagara, immediately beyond our bathroom. And when finally all the waterfalls had stopped, and the enchanted hunters were sound asleep, the avenue under the window of my insomnia, to the west of my wake—a staid, eminently residential, dignified alley of huge trees—degenerated into the despicable haunt of gigantic trucks roaring through the wet and windy night."

In the first antemeridian hours there is a lull. The sky pales. A breeze sighs. A bird discreetly twitters. Lolita wakes up and yawns (a childish, cozy, warm yawn). Humbert feigns sleep.

LOLITA (*sitting up, looking at him*) What d'you know! I thought you got another room. Hey! Wake up!

Humbert gives a mediocre imitation of that process.

LOLITA I never heard you come in. Oh, you're handsome in bed, Hum. Is that cot comfortable?

HUMBERT Awful.

LOLITA Come and sit here. Shall we eat that fruit in the brown bag? You need a shave, pricklepuss.

HUMBERT Good morning, Lolita.

LOLITA My tan is much darker that yours. Say, I have a suggestion. Are you listening?

HUMBERT Yes?

LOLITA It's something we did at the camp, Charlie and me. It's fun.

HUMBERT Yes?

LOLITA Gosh, how your heart is thumping! Shouldn't you see a doctor? You aren't dying?

HUMBERT I am dying of curiosity. What was that suggestion?

LOLITA   It's playing a game. A game we played in the
    woods—when we should have been picking berries. I did
    it strictly for kicks, but oh well, it was sort of fun. It's
    a game lots of kids play nowadays. Kind of fad. Still
    don't get it? You're dense, aren't you?

HUMBERT   I'm dying.

LOLITA   It's—sure you can't guess?

HUMBERT   I can't.

LOLITA   It's not tiddledywinks, and it's not Russian
    roulette.

HUMBERT   I'm a poor guesser.

With a burst of rough glee she puts her mouth to his ear
(could one reproduce this hot moist sound, the tickle and
the buzz, the vibration, the thunder of her whisper?).
    She draws back. Kneeling above recumbent Humbert (who
is invisible except for a twitching toe), she contemplates
him expectantly. Her humid lips and sly slit eyes seem to
anticipate and prompt an assent.

HUMBERT'S VOICE   I don't know what game you
    children played.

In an eager gesture, she brushes the hair off her forehead and
applies herself again to his tingling ear.

HUMBERT'S VOICE   (faintly) I never played that
    game.

LOLITA'S VOICE   Like me to show you?

HUMBERT   If it's not too dangerous. If it's not too difficult. If it's not too—*Ah, mon Dieu!*

CUT TO:

Various Rooms in the Enchanted Hunters
The CAMERA glides from room to room at dawn, with some of the guests still fast asleep. The purpose of these shots is to construct a series of situations contrasting with the atmosphere in Room 342. The movement of the CAMERA reveals the following scenes, all of very brief duration:

Room 13:   Mr. Potts, the hotel clerk, old, chubby, and bald, is awakened by his alarm clock, which he knocks over in his fussy attempt to stop its ringing.

Room 180:   Dr. and Mrs. Braddock—he snoring lustily; she is awakened by two pigeons on the window sill.

Room 423:   The playwright Quilty, dead to the world, sprawls prone among the emblems of drunkenness.

Room 342: (balcony) Pigeons. Early sunlight effects. A truck rumbles by below. From the inside of the room comes the laughter of a child (Lolita!).

Room 344:   The laughter of a child in the neighboring room rouses Dr. Boyd, who looks at his watch and smiles.

Room 442:   A very large woman, Miss Beard, has risen and indulges in some ponderous exercises causing the flowers to shake in her small room.

Room 342:   Lolita, sitting up in her tumbled bed, looks up at the loud ceiling. She is messily consuming a peach. A banana skin hangs from the edge of the bed table. The cot is empty. Humbert is in the bathroom, the door of which is ajar. The faucet whines.

Room 242: Mr. Rose is shaving in the bathroom. The faucet in the bathroom above whines. Mrs. Rose urges her daughter, a dark-haired child Lolita's age, to get up.

Murals in the dining room: The hunters are still in a trance.

Corridor on third floor: Negro maids load a wagon with linen.

The morning grows in brightness and blare. The elevator is active. It is now around 9 A.M. One of the maids attempts to open the door of 342. Humbert's nervous snarl from within.

CUT TO:

Room 342
Lolita combs her hair before the mirror.

HUMBERT'S VOICE   I love you. I adore you ...

LOLITA   Oh, leave me alone now. We must get dressed.

HUMBERT'S VOICE   Lolita, Lolita, Lolita! Please, not yet. Oh, my darling. This is——

CUT TO:

Hotel Dining Room

DR. BRADDOCK   (*pointing out details of mural to the Rose family*) This is paradise, or at least a pagan shadow of paradise. Note those ecstatic flowers and things sprouting everywhere. In this corner we have one of the enchanted hunters courting a young nymph. The coloration of the sky is dreamlike. I knew well Lewis Ruskin who painted this remarkable mural. He was a gentle soul, a melancholy drawing master who eventually became the head of a select girls' school in Briceland. He developed a romantic attachment for one of his young charges and committed suicide when she left his school. She is now married to a missionary.

MRS. ROSE   How very sad. Don't you just love those three maidens dancing around the sleeping hunter? And that shaggy animal with the mauve horn?

MRS. ROSE' LITTLE DAUGHTER   Why has one of the girls a bandage on her leg?

CUT TO:

Lounge to Dining Room
Humbert, followed by Lolita, drifts in. She acquires a movie magazine which she reads throughout breakfast, and continues to read as they trail out, and reads it in the lounge while Humbert is paying the bill.

A VOICE   Hullo there, Lolita!

She looks around. There is no one. Humbert joins her. Old Tom carries out the bags.

CUT TO:

The Highway to Lepingsville
They drive in silence. A queer dullness has replaced Lolita's cheerfulness.

HUMBERT   (*attempting small talk*) My, my. I wonder what Mrs. Chatfield would say if she discovered the things her pretty Phyllis did with your filthy Charlie.

LOLITA   (*making a weeping grimace*) Look, let us get off the subject.

Silence. Some landscape.

HUMBERT   Why are you fidgeting like that? What is the matter?

LOLITA   Nothing, you brute.

HUMBERT   You what?

She turns away.

They drive on in silence. "Cold spiders of panic crawled down my back. This was an orphan . . ."

CUT TO:

Receding Road

LOLITA   Oh, a squashed squirrel! What a shame.

HUMBERT   (*hopefully*) Yes, isn't it? The little animals are imprudent. You know, there should be——

LOLITA   Stop at the next gas station. I want to go to the washroom.

HUMBERT   Righto. Tummy-ache?

LOLITA   (*smiling sweetly at him*) You chump, you
creep, you revolting character. I was a daisy-fresh girl
and look what you've done to me. I ought to call the
cops and tell them you raped me. Oh, you dirty, dirty
old man!

Humbert frowns, sweats, glances at her askance.

LOLITA   (*wincing and making a sizzling sound as she
intakes through parted lips*) You hurt me. You've torn
something inside.

CUT TO:

A Filling Station
She scrambles out and disappears. Slowly, lovingly, the old
mechanic soaps and wipes the windshield, etc. Lolita reappears.

LOLITA   Look, give me some dimes and nickles. I want
to call Mother at that hospital. What's the number?

HUMBERT   Get in. You can't call.

LOLITA   Why?

HUMBERT   Get in and slam the door.

The old garage man beams. They swing onto the highway.

LOLITA   Why can't I call my mother if I want to?

HUMBERT   Because your mother is dead.

CUT TO:

Lepingsville—a Travel Agency on Main Street
A thick smear crayon traces across a map the itinerary which
Humbert and Lolita will follow through three or four
mountain states, to Beardsley, Idaho. Besides the folding map,
they are given a strip map and a tour book.

CUT TO:

Humbert and Lolita Shopping in Lepingsville
The purchases are: a beribboned box of chocolates, comic
books, toilet articles, a manicure set, a travel clock, a ring
with a real topaz, field glasses, a portable radio, chewing gum,
a transparent raincoat, various playsuits and summer frocks.
She remains rather sullen throughout though some of the
purchases do provoke a transient gleam in her gloom.

CUT TO:

A Forest Road at Nightfall
They have stopped by the side of the road.

HUMBERT   We must have taken the wrong turning.
    This is awful.

He gets the map and a torch light.

LOLITA   Give me that map.

HUMBERT   We should have turned left half an hour
    ago and taken 42 south, not north.

LOLITA   We? Leave me out of it.

HUMBERT   (*over her shoulder*) I am sure we'll find
    some place to stop, if we just drive on.

[116]

He nuzzles her tentatively.

LOLITA   (*flinching*) Leave me alone. I despise you. You
      deceived me about Mother. You took advantage of me.

CUT TO:

We see the Car moving on
This is the first, rather ominous, lap in their trip. Things will
pick up, however—and then degenerate again.

It is assumed that Humbert and Lolita are traversing by car
a distance of some three thousand miles, including side trips,
from Lepingsville (which is anywhere between Massachusetts
and Minnesota) westward through several mountain states to
Beardsley, a college town in Idaho. Their journey is a leisurely,
sightseeing tour, so that it takes them not less than two or
three weeks to reach, in mid-September, their destination. All
along their route there is an evolution of the motel theme,
illustrated by six examples beginning with the modest log
cabin (Acme Cabins), through cottages in a row (Baskerville Cottages), garage-connected units (Crest Court), fused
units (Dymple Manor), and the patio-and-pool type (Eden
Lodge), to the fancy two-story affair (Foxcreek Ranch), a
gradation which, if pursued further, would lead us back to the
country hotel. There is also a (shorter) series of eating places,
from the breakfast counter of the Truckers Welcome, through
the coffee-shop type, to the more or less smart restaurant.

While the accommodations improve, and their pretentions
climb, Lolita's attitude takes an opposite, downward, course,
starting with a forlorn semblance of affection and passing
through a gamut of deterioration, to end in the wretchedness
of their last night before reaching Beardsley.

We have now put up at The Humble Log Cabin, where Humbert and Lolita will conclude a pathetic pact—soon to be broken.

CUT TO:

Acme Cabins—a Modest Cabin, One of Five, Higgledy-piggledy in a Pine Forest
None has a bath. The separate privy is garlanded with wild roses. A brisk, buxom, unkempt woman shows our tired travelers the wood-burning stove and the two dissimilar beds, separable by a curtain on rings. There is a Bible on the chest of drawers. A fly buzzes drowsily. Above Humbert's bed there is the picture of a girl garlanded with wild roses.

Humbert, in his curtained-off section, sits on the bed with his face between his fists in mournful meditation. Presently, he puts out the light and lies down; silence. The moon rises, a disturbed fly buzzes and is still again. Humbert lies in the mottled dark with eyes open, his arms under his nape.

A child sob sounds and is followed by more. He sits up, listening. The curtain is drawn aside.

Lolita with tears streaming down her face, her nightgown white and infantine in the moonlight, comes to be comforted. He gently caresses her hair, as she weeps on his shoulder.

HUMBERT   I beseech you not to cry. I love you. I cannot exist without you. Everything will be all right.

LOLITA   (*with a snuffle and a wail*) Nothing will ever be all right.

HUMBERT   I'm sure we are going to be very happy, you and I.

[118]

LOLITA   But everything has *changed,* all of a sudden. Everything was so—oh, I don't know—normal: the camp, and the lake, and Charlie, and the girls, and the —oh, everything. And now there is no camp, and no Ramsdale, nothing!

There is the patter of some little night beast on the roof.

HUMBERT   I don't want you to cry. We'll see things, we'll go places.

LOLITA   There's no place to go back to.

HUMBERT   We'll find a new home.

LOLITA   But there's no old one. And I've left all my things there.

HUMBERT   What, for instance?

LOLITA   My roller skates, my—oh, lots of things.

HUMBERT   You silly darling, why didn't you tell me in Lepingsville?

LOLITA   (*tearfully*) I forgot.

HUMBERT   We'll get every blessed thing you want. It's over two thousand miles to Beardsley but we've got a month before the fall term begins. We can dawdle as much as you want.

LOLITA   But what next? Oh, where is that handkerchief?

HUMBERT   Next you'll go to school in Beardsley, and have a wonderful time there. I love you. I'm also going to cry if you don't stop. Remember, I'll die if you ever leave me.

LOLITA   Leave you? You know perfectly well I have nowhere to go.

CUT TO:

Baskerville Cottages
Ten white-washed cottages in a row, with a vast well-kept lawn in front, separating them from the highway.

Lolita and Humbert in a Leafy Spot not far from their cottage. Humbert with a book on the grass. Lolita in an old garden swing, swinging gently.

HUMBERT   You have been a very sweet child so far. It would be a pity to break the precious rhythm we have now established. I suggest we spend another night here, in this fairy-tale cabin. We shall ramble and read. Do you know, these notes on Edgar Poe that I have prepared for Beardsley College always remind me of Ramsdale and the first time I touched you. Come here, sit down beside me. I'll read you my favorite poem.

LOLITA   (*in the swing, just behind him*) I want to sit here.

HUMBERT   All right, but don't make it creak. I want you to follow very closely the intonation, the inner construction of these lines.
It was night in the lonesome October
Of my most immemorial year
Marvelous emphasis on "immemorial." Makes you step up from one dim rim to a dimmer one.

It was hard by the dim lake of Auber,
In the misty mid region of Weir

> Notice how nicely the "dim" is read back and becomes "mid"—"misty mid region"?

> *(The swing creaks.)*

HUMBERT   Darling, please don't do that. I skip a few stanzas. Now listen again:

Thus I pacified Psyche and kissed her
And tempted her out of her gloom . . .
And we passed to the end of the vista,
But were stopped by the door of a tomb
. . . And I said: "What is written, sweet sister? . . .
She replied: Ulalume, Ulalume!

LOLITA   I think that's rather corny.

HUMBERT   Really? What exactly do you object to?

LOLITA   Vista-sister. That's like Lolita-sweeter.

HUMBERT   Oh, that's true. A very fine observation.

(A more or less tame rabbit stops, nibbles, lopes on.)

HUMBERT   In my class you'd get an A-plus and a kiss. But what I'm really driving at is that there is a certain intonation in this poem which is so much more original and mysterious than the rather trivial romanticism of Annabel Lee. *(He turns his head and notices the swing is empty.)*

HUMBERT   *(getting up to his feet)* Lolita!

(She has disappeared)

HUMBERT   Lolita, where are you hiding?

He looks for her among the trees and shrubs. He is in a state of distress and distraction hardly warranted by the circumstances. (She has wandered away in dim-smiling, stooping pursuit of the soft elusive rabbit)

HUMBERT   (*emerging from a thicket*) Lolita!

She is crouching behind the circumspect bunny. A very low-class young couple with an unattractive baby are on the back porch of a cabin. They talk to Lolita. The young man is not unlike (and should be played by the same actor as) Lolita's future husband.

THE YOUNG MAN   I guess he doesn't want to be
     caught.

Humbert, excited and angry, appears on the scence.

HUMBERT   Will you please come at once. I've been
     calling you for hours. This is preposterous.
          (*Does not quite know what he is saying.*)

Lolita turns and walks back to their cabin, followed by Humbert and the CAMERA. She stops near their parked car, and jiggles the door handle.

LOLITA   Unlock, please.

HUMBERT   Darling, you must forgive me.

LOLITA   You've insulted me in front of those people.

HUMBERT   I lost my head. I was reading a poem. I got
     the nightmare notion that you had disappeared for good

—that perhaps you never existed. Don't be mad at me, my love. I'll unlock if you like, but don't be mad. Your mother once told me that when you were quite small and wanted to sulk, you'd get into the family car all alone.

LOLITA   I don't care. You can't do this to me.

HUMBERT   I know, I know. I'm asking your pardon. It won't happen again. I'm a fool. I thought you were gone.

LOLITA   I've nowhere to go.

CUT TO:

Breakfast Counter in a Diner Called TRUCKERS WELCOME
A very plain place with a deer head and adman's visions of celestial sundaes on the wall. At the counter, Lolita has Humbert on her right and a tremendous trucker with hairy forearms on her left. The trucker and Lolita wear identical clothes: dungarees and T-shirts. The man is messily finishing his meal. Humbert and Lolita are waiting for theirs.

CUT TO:

Lolita, Humbert, Driving on
The road is bordered by hilly farmlands and then winds through sparsely settled country interspersed with pine groves.

CUT TO:

Crest Court—a semicircle of stucco units connected by narrow garages
The lawn in front is shaded by ample maples. Inside, two

identical pictures (stylized dahlias) hang over the twin beds. The hideous drone of an air-conditioning apparatus provides a constant sonic background.

CUT TO:

Long Shot—Humbert and Lolita Arriving
It is the ordinary procedure. They both get out of the car in front of the office. The woman who runs the motel cries out, "I'll be with you in a moment," as she hurriedly escorts some other people back to the office from the room they have seen. It is now Humbert's and Lolita's turn. They follow the sidewalk in the wake of the bustling woman. She shows them the room. Humbert nods his head. Listless, Lolita drops into a low chair. Humbert follows the woman back to the office and registers there.

HUMBERT   Where can I get some soft drinks round here?

THE WOMAN   It's just one block down the road.

Humbert walks out to follow her directions but then thinks better of it and returns to the room, where Lolita is sprawling in the chair with a magazine.

HUMBERT   We'll be going out in five minutes for a bite. Do lay aside that old magazine and come talk to me.

Lolita scans magazine without replying.

HUMBERT   Do you hear me, darling? I want a little chat with you, *mon petit chat*. Please.

[124]

LOLITA   If you give me a dime. From now on I am coin
    operated.

She continues to read.

    Humbert, who has taken off his shirt, notices the approach
of the motel woman and steps into the bathroom. The woman
enters bringing a jug of ice cubes.

THE WOMAN   There. You can have a nice cold drink,
    dearie. Long way from home?

LOLITA   Home? Yes, I guess so. Very long way.

WOMAN   Must be fun to travel all alone with your
    daddy?

LOLITA   Oh, I dunno——

WOMAN   Depends on what you call fun?

LOLITA   Uh-huh.

WOMAN   Left your mama up at the farm?

LOLITA   Uhn-uhn. We don't have a farm.

WOMAN   Get along with your daddy?

LOLITA   Yah.

WOMAN   You don't talk the way he does. I mean, he
    talks foreign, and you don't.

LOLITA   Oh, well—I went to school in this country.

WOMAN   And he didn't? Is he French Canadian?

LOLITA   Sort of.

WOMAN   Look, there's a Canadian couple living across the road. Maybe you'd like to talk to them?

LOLITA   Why?

HUMBERT   (*from the threshold of the bathroom*) Yes —why indeed?

WOMAN   Oh, I thought you had gone out for a drink.

HUMBERT   By the way, can you stop that ventilator, or whatever you call it? I can't stand that whirr.

CUT TO:

Another Stretch of Road
For the first time sagebrush and juniper appear. There is some uncertainty whether it is a bank of clouds or a range of mountains that have started looming just above the horizon. By the side of the road, a granite obelisk commemorates a bloody battle—the defeat of Blue Bull.

A Crowded Coffee Shop
A hard-working harried young waitress is doing her best to satisfy too many customers.

LOLITA   (*to Humbert*) Give me a coin for the juke box. Oh, they have my song.

She starts the juke box. The following song is produced:

Lolita, Lolita, Lolita!
For ever tonight we must part:
Because separation is sweeter
Than clasping a ghost to one's heart.

Because it's a maddening summer,
Because the whole night is in bloom,
Because you're in love with a strummer
Who brings his guitar to your room.

You know he's a clown and a cheater,
You know I am tender and true—
But *he* is now singing, Lolita,
The songs I've been making for you!

CUT TO:

The Route now offers spectacular scenery
as it snakes up a gigantic mountainside. At the top of the pass,
tourists take pictures and feed the marmots. In the next valley
we inspect the collection of frontier lore in a Ghost Town
museum. We have a little trouble when the car stalls on a
steep incline but some kind youths help. The radiator grill is
plastered with dead butterflies.

CUT TO:

A Dirt Road in a Canyon
Humbert pulls up at the bloomy and lush wayside.

HUMBERT   I should not have attempted to take a short
      cut. We're lost.

LOLITA   Ask that nut with the net over there.

[127]

The Butterfly Hunter. His name is Vladimir Nabokov. A fritillary settles with outspread wings on a tall flower. Nabokov snaps it up with a sweep of his net. Humbert walks toward him. With a nip of finger and thumb through a fold of the marquisette Nabokov dispatches his capture and works the dead insect out of the netbag onto the palm of his hand.

HUMBERT   Is that a rare specimen?

NABOKOV   A specimen cannot be common or rare, it can only be poor or perfect.

HUMBERT   Could you direct me——

NABOKOV   You meant "rare species." This is a good specimen of a rather scarce subspecies.

HUMBERT   I see. Could you please tell me if this road leads to Dympleton?

NABOKOV   I haven't the vaguest idea. I saw some loggers (*pointing*) up there. They might know.

CUT TO:

Dymple Manor—twenty units firmly fused together in a Row
The screen doors never cease banging as people come in and out, and the only way to confound one's neighbor's canned music is to start one's own full blast. Sprinklers irrigate the parched-looking lawn and its border of trembling petunias. In the adjacent lot a bulldozer is at work, and another motel is rising.

LOLITA   Give me a quarter for the TV.

HUMBERT   It's free, my pet, in this, as they say, joint.

A notice under glass says PETS ACCEPTED.

LOLITA   I need a quarter anyway.

HUMBERT   My pet must earn it.

CUT TO:

The Television Screen
A commercial is melting:

A FRUITY VOICE   . . . soft, soft as the bloom on a
     peach.

SUPREMELY HAPPY ANNOUNCER   And now we
     return to Act One of *The Nymphet*

LOLITA'S VOICE   Oh, I saw it at home last winter. It's
     good.

On the TV screen, an art collector is seen examining a minia-
ture statue: a tiny bronze nude.

HIS SUBDUED NARRATIONAL VOICE   I had
     bought it on a hunch; but now, as I stroked each curve,
     I knew it was a unique masterpiece.

CLOSE-UP of the statuette, which is called "Playing Hooky."
A teen-age girl is about to take a dip, her dress and school
books are lying at the foot of a gnarled willow.

NARRATIVE UNDERVOICE CONTINUES   I knew
     that the artist who made it was traveling in a distant

country with his young wife. A strange urge possessed me. Next day I was flying over the jungle.

HUMBERT'S VOICE   Must we look at this trash?

LOLITA'S VOICE   It's not trash. It will get quite exciting. He finds the girl and he shoots her.

CUT TO:

High Altitude
We stop at Sapphire Lake. Snow banks and wild flowers. Two boys from another car engage Lolita in a snowball fight. Humbert, who has incongruously put on rubbers, slips on an icy patch and ignominiously lands on his back. Lolita and the boys laugh at his discomfiture. A scenic drive takes our travelers to the Pueblo dwellings. A rodeo is advertised in the next town.

CUT TO:

Eden Lodge
We are now in the patio-and-pool belt. The arrangement of fused whitewashed units brackets a square of green grounds with a heated swimming pool in the middle. The rooms are smarter and more expensive than at Crest or Dymple; unfortunately, a tented roller-skate rink on the opposite side of the road impairs Eden's elegancy with a sustained blare of rowdy music.

In the Room

LOLITA   (*reading a notice*) Children free. Goody-goody.

HUMBERT   (*laughing tenderly*) No quarter tonight, free child.

[130]

LOLITA   That's what you think. From now on *this* child is paid half a dollar.

HUMBERT   My Persian peach.

LOLITA   And moreover—moreover you must promise you'll let me go roller-skating—no, wait a sec—it's not only that, but you must promise you'll not supervise me —I mean, you may wait outside, or at the chuck wagon, but the inside is reserved for teen-agers. See?

HUMBERT   My carissa, my liquidambar, my early delicious.

CUT TO:

Swimming Pool
At poolside Lolita (satin pants, shirred bra) and two other nymphets (one dark, with a striped ball in her scanty lap, the other fair, with a long scar on her leg) recline. A lad of their age, in bathing trunks, sits on the cement brink, paying not the slightest attention to the three maidens.

FAIR   (*in response to Lolita's index finger*) Rock climbing in Pink Pillar Park. Skinned my fanny too. That's a cute bracelet you've got.

LOLITA   Thank you.

DARK   You can't be Spanish, Lolita?

LOLITA   (*smile, shrug*)

FAIR   (to DARK) Are your folks like mine—playing cards all day?

[131]

DARK   My father is an admiral, and my mother's an actress.

FAIR   Good for you. (*pause*) That character there (*pointing with her bare toe at owlish Humbert, who at some distance beyond the pool is sitting in a shadow-dappled garden chair*), I know why *he* wears sunglasses.

(Dark girl and Lolita exchange a glance, and both laugh.)

DARK   It's her dad, bright kid.

FAIR   I'm sorry.

All three wince as the lad dives, splashing them.

FAIR   And who's the nitwit?

DARK   He belongs to this motor court.

Humbert, in the dappled distance, raises his hand beckoning Lolita. She makes a grimace of resignation, and leaves the poolside.

DARK   (*to Fair*) I bet her folks are divorced.

FAIR   (*to Dark*) Yah. She looks like one of those mixed-up kids you see on TV.

CUT TO:

Poolside

HUMBERT   (*closing his book*) I see from this point of vantage they have finished cleaning up our room. I therefore suggest we retire for a brief siesta, my love.

LOLITA   I want a hamburger first.

HUMBERT   And then a humburger.

LOLITA   Those two bitch girls are watching us.

HUMBERT   A propos: I don't mind your playing with girls of your age. In fact, I rather welcome it if I can be present. You may exchange wisecracks with them to your heart's content. But I must repeat: be careful.

LOLITA   Telling me what to say—huh?

HUMBERT   Telling you what not to say.

CUT TO:

The Motel Room

HUMBERT   Now let me rub this in. I may well be a middle-aged morals offender, *d'accord,* but *you* are a minor female who has impaired the morals of an adult in a respectable inn. I go to jail—*d'accord.* But what happens to you, neglected incorrigible orphan? Let me tell you: a nice grim matron takes away your fancy clothes, your lipsticks, your life. For me, it is jail. But for you, little waif, it is the correctional school, the bleak reformatory, the juvenile detention home where you knit things, and sing hymns, and have rancid pancakes on Sundays. Oh, horrible! My poor wayward girl (come, give me a kiss) should realize, I think, that under the circumstances she'd better be very careful, and not talk to strangers too freely. What were you giggling about with those two girls?

CUT TO:

A Roadside Sign: PINK PILLAR NATIONAL MONUMENT. Another sign further on: SADDLE HORSES. PERSONALIZED TOURS.

DISSOLVE TO:

A Slow Cavalcade of Tourists
weaving along a bridle trail, topped by digitate and phallic cliffs. Lolita is bobbing at a walking pace immediately behind the leader, a lanky ranger who keeps turning to her and kidding the cocky lass. A fat dude rancher in a flowery shirt rides behind her, then come two small boys, then a Mrs. Hopson, and then Humbert.

Edda Hopson (her name is on her back) takes advantage of a widening in the path to fall back and engage reluctant Humbert in polite conversation (oh, shade of Charlotte!).

MRS. HOPSON   What a lovely child you've got! I kept admiring her last night in the lounge. Those cheekbones! That virgin bloom on her arms and legs! I'm a bit of an artist, and in fact have exposed. Keep her pure! I do hope she has a good heart. I used to hurt my parents as a savage hurts dumb animals. Is she kind to you? Does she love you?

HUMBERT   No.

MRS. HOPSON   Ah, teen-agers are dreadfully cruel. And such a little beauty! A word of advice: don't let that redhaired brute of a ranger tease her the way he is doing. I rode with him alone once, and he exhibited his —well, emotion most shamelessly. I must say I thought it rather thick: knowing I was a divorcee and taking advantage.

CUT TO:

A Fairly Good Restaurant

Tablecloths and napkins. Waiters. A three-man orchestra. Lolita and Humbert sit at a table in shaded light.

LOLITA (*to Humbert*) What's a roast caponette?

HUMBERT Chicken.

LOLITA No. I'll have the charcoal-broiled filet mignon.

The orchestra plays "Lolita, Lolita, Lolita." Humbert has ordered half a bottle of wine.

LOLITA Give me some.

HUMBERT If nobody's looking. Well, here's to your health, my life and my bride.

LOLITA Okay, okay.

HUMBERT I'm so anxious to make you happy. Just don't know what to suggest. I'm rather awkward and sometimes a brute. But I adore every inch of you. I'd like to kiss your kidneys and fondle your liver. Tell me, what shall we do tomorrow? Let's stay here a couple of days longer and take in Phantom Lake and perhaps hire a boat there. Would you like that?

LOLITA A boat? What do you know about boats?

HUMBERT Why are you laughing?

LOLITA I just remembered. One day we went in the rowboat, Phyl, Agnes, and me, and we found a cove, and went for a swim, and Charlie came out of the wood just like that. And of course he was not supposed to go swimming with us, and Phyllis said——

THE WAITER   Would the young lady like some more milk?

LOLITA   Yes, I guess so.

HUMBERT   So what did Phyllis say?

LOLITA   Nothing.

HUMBERT   I had hoped I was getting another racy account of your camp activities.

LOLITA   No, that's all.

Three days are spent in this region, and some side trips are made. Humbert photographs Lolita among the rocks of the Devil's Paint Box—hot springs, baby geysers, bubbling mud, pouting puddles. Another trip takes them to Christmas Tree Cavern, a deep damp place where Humbert shivers and is rude to the guide. A long drive toward a disappointing objective—the display of a local lady's home-made sculptures—does not improve Lolita's mood. She feigns gagging. They traverse an incredibly barren and boring desert. Timbered hills rise again.

CUT TO:

Foxcreek Ranch
This is the last and most pretentious motel of the series, a two-story affair, very fancy and ugly, in the heart of the train and truck traffic. The office is brightly illumined. The time is rather late at night.

THE MANAGER   Well, all I have left is this one room
     with a double bed.

Lolita is examining some Indian souvenirs on the counter.

LOLITA   (*to Humbert, who is about to register*) I want
     this money purse.

HUMBERT   Wait a moment, my dear.

LOLITA   I want this purse.

HUMBERT   *Mais c'est si laid.*

LOLITA   *Si laid* or not *si laid*—I want it.

HUMBERT   All right, all right.

MANAGER   (*giving Humbert his change*) Fifteen, and
     —let me see—three ninety-five for this. One silver dollar
     and one new nickel. Would the young lady like her
     monogram upon it?

LOLITA   Yes. It's D.H.

MANAGER   Aha. Very well. Where did my old dad put
     those initials? Dad! Oh, here they are.

LOLITA   D.H. Dolores Haze.

Humbert has started to write his name on a register slip. He
has got as far as "Humbert Hu." With great presence of mind
he changes "u" to "a," and adds "ze."

MANAGER   Ask your dad for that dollar, Dolores.
     That's a tongue twister—dollar doll—isn't it?

[137]

CUT TO:

Front of Hacienda
The manager shows Humbert where to park.

CUT TO:

Room
Wall-to-wall carpeting and floor-to-ceiling picture windows; dressing alcove; ceramic-tiled bath; trucks and trains accompany the dialogue.

HUMBERT   That "Haze" was a bad slip of your adorable little tongue. While we put up at hotels, you are—remember—Dolores Humbert. Let's keep "Haze" for the reformatory.

LOLITA   Meaning that school at Beardsley?

HUMBERT   You're going to an extremely good private school at Beardsley. But one hot whisper to a girl friend, one stupid boast, may send me to jail and you to a juvenile detention home.

LOLITA   By the way, you said "private." Is it a girls' school?

HUMBERT   Yes.

LOLITA   Then I'm not going there. I want to go to an ordinary public school.

HUMBERT   Let's not fight and argue tonight. I'm fagged out. We have to start quite early tomorrow. Please, Dolly Humbert.

[138]

LOLITA   I loathe your name. It's a clown's name: Humlet Hambert. Omelette Hamburg.

HUMBERT   Or plain "Hamlet." I daresay, you hate me even more than my name. Oh, Lolita, if you knew what you are doing to me. Some day you'll regret.

LOLITA   That's right. Just go clowning on and on.

HUMBERT   Well, let's struggle with these blinds. The war with Venice. I can't do anything with these slats and slits.

LOLITA   I'm not listening to you, you know.

HUMBERT   Pity. This is our last night on the road. I wonder what kind of house the Beardsley people have prepared for us. I hope it's brick and ivy.

LOLITA   I could not care less.

HUMBERT   But don't you think it has been an enchanting journey? Tell me, what did you like best of all? I think, yesterday's canyon, eh? I think I've never seen such iridescent rocks.

LOLITA   I think iridescent rocks stink.

HUMBERT   (*affecting a good-natured laugh*) Have it your way.

She takes off her shoes. Her movements are slumber-slow.

LOLITA   I'm thirsty.

HUMBERT   There's ice in this jug.

Tinkle.

LOLITA   (*hazily*) I want a soda.

HUMBERT   Shall I bring you one from the Coke
    dispenser?

LOLITA   (*yawns and nods*)

HUMBERT   Grape? Cherry?

LOLITA   Cherry. No, make it grape.

She yawns.

CUT TO:

Spacious Patio, Neon-flooded Solitude
Humbert walks to the vending machine which is outside the
motel office. Dime. Bottle. Repeat performance. He opens
both bottles on the cap-bite.

AN OLD MAN'S VOICE   The missus thirsty?

It is the deaf old father of the hotel manager sitting and
smoking in the shadows.

HUMBERT   I beg your pardon?

OLD MAN   Women sure get thirsty.

HUMBERT   It's my daughter. . . .

OLD MAN	What's that?

HUMBERT	. . . who wants a drink.

OLD MAN	No, thank you, very kind of you.

HUMBERT   (*after a moment's hesitation*) Well, good
night.

OLD MAN   My wife was also like that—but *her* drink
was beer.

Chuckles, mumbles, expectorates in the dark.

CUT TO:

Humbert
walking back to his door with the two bottles. He reaches
the door. He has not got the key. As he frees his hand to
knock, the telephone rings somewhere in an adjacent room
and for a moment the shadow of a past combination of
memorable details is imposed upon the present (". . . better
come quick . . .") Humbert taps gently on the door. No answer.

HUMBERT   (*not too loud*) Lolita!

No answer. He taps again, then peers through the slits of the
Venetian blind. A blurry light is on in the room. Lolita, half
undressed, lies supine on the bed, fast asleep.

It is hopeless. Humbert is disinclined to get the manager
to come and unlock: the nymphet's sleep is not that of an
acceptable child.

CUT TO:

Humbert
mouth open, asleep in the car. It is dawn. From one of the
motel rooms there gradually emerges a big family—sleepy
children, portable icebox, accepted pet, crib—and fills a big
station wagon which has the stickers of various resorts and
natural marvels affixed to it: a summary also of Humbert's
honeymoon. One of the children turns on the radio.

Act Three

Beardsley School
A private school for girls at Beardsley, Idaho. It is a sunny spring day. There are catkins in all the vases. We are in the music room of the school. It is here that the drama classes are held. Several girls, including Lolita, mostly in gym suits, some barefoot, sit around, some on the floor. Miss Cormorant, a lean faded Lesbian, is discussing the play which they will stage at the Spring Festival of Arts.

MISS CORMORANT   For our Spring Festival next month, we are going to do a play by Clare Quilty. When I taught at Onyx, Mr. Cue, as we called him, would sometimes drive over from Briceland to direct a dance pantomime. The girls adored him. One day he told me that he and a famous painter, the late Lewis Ruskin, were engaged in writing a play for children. Eventually, Mr. Quilty published it under the intriguing title, *The Enchanted Hunters.* And this is the play we are going to do. Why are you laughing, Lolita? Did I say anything hilarious?

LOLITA   No, Miss Cormorant.

CORMORANT   The play is a charming fantasy. Several hunters are lost in a wood, and a strange girl they meet puts them into a kind of trance. They fraternize with mythical creatures. Of course, later the girl turns out to be a student at a nearby Institute for Extra-Sensorial Studies, and all ends quite plausibly. Mr. Quilty will be giving a lecture at Beardsley College at the end of this month, and I'm sure he'll help us to rehearse.

CUT TO:

Beardsley College (A coeducational institution where Humbert Humbert teaches)
The flowers that were budding in the first scene are now opening. A shrill whirring bell rings through the corridors. Students are leaving the classroom, where Humbert is collecting his notes. Miss Shatzki, an intense unkempt young woman in a formless sweater, speaks to him.

HUMBERT   Yes, I see what you mean, Miss Shatzki.

MISS SHATZKI   I would also like to ask you about Poe's other love affairs. Don't you think——

CUT TO:

College Corridor with moving sunlight at the far end
Humbert walks down this long passage toward the exit. At one point various publicity items are tacked onto a cork board hanging on the wall. Humbert's glance passes across:

MISS EMMA KING, PIANO LESSONS

SPRING IS HERE—SAY IT WITH ADELE'S DAF-FODILS AT THE CAMPUS FLOWER SHOP

FOUND: : A GIRL'S LEATHER BELT

[144]

FRIDAY, 8 P.M., MAIN AUDITORIUM
FAMOUS PLAYWRIGHT CLARE QUILTY
WILL LECTURE ON THE LOVE OF ART

CUT TO:

Campus—Humbert
walks across the turfy expanse toward the parking lot, a small group issues from the college library. An instructor of English and a couple of students have been conducting a distinguished visitor, Quilty, and his constant companion, Vivian Dark-bloom, on a tour through the stacks. Vivian is a stylish, bob-haired, lanky lady in a well-tailored suit, with striking exotic features marred by a certain coarseness of epiderm. The following scene is accompanied by a strong spring wind blowing across the campus.

INSTRUCTOR   (*to Quilty*)
   Next week the Department of Anthropology is arranging a special exhibition in the Rare Books department. It will feature some rugs, and, I think, sacred pictures, which Professor and Mrs. Brooks brought back from Moscow.

QUILTY   Fascinating.

INSTRUCTOR   (*noticing Humbert, who is passing by*)
   Oh, Professor Humbert!

Humbert stops.

INSTRUCTOR   Mr. Quilty, this is Professor Humbert, our visiting lecturer in Comparative Literature.

[145]

QUILTY   I don't think we have actually met—or have
    we? Seen you a couple of times in Ramsdale and else-
    where. Happy occasions.

He mumbles and smirks.

VIVIAN DARKBLOOM   (*very distinctly*)
And I am Vivian Darkbloom.

QUILTY   (*his sparse hair and necktie stirring in the
    strong wind*) My collaborator, my evening shadow. Her
    name looks like an anagram. But she's a real woman—
    or anyway a real person. You're an inch taller than me,
    aren't you, m'dear?

VIVIAN   (*training her brilliant smile upon Humbert*)
    My niece Mona goes to Beardsley School with your
    daughter.

HUMBERT   Step.

QUILTY   (*addressing the instructor and the two stu-
    dents*) You know the first thing people usually say when
    I'm introduced to them is how much they like, or simply
    adore, my *Nymphet* on TV.

HUMBERT   I do have a vague recollection . . .

QUILTY   Good for you. I often wonder what is tech-
    nically more vague—a vague recollection or a vague
    premonition.
                        (*to Vivian*)
    This is a philosophic question, my dear, way above your
    pretty head. Ghouls of the past or phantoms of the
    future—which do we choose?

HUMBERT   Some of my best friends are phantoms.

QUILTY   Sense of humor, I see. What a wind! *Quel vent!* Lucky I'm not wearing my toopee. Have a cigarette.

Humbert declines.

QUILTY   It should have been a Drome, but it is not. It's a very special Spanish brand made especially for me, for my urgent needs.
                    (*Dissolves in ghoulish
                    giggles.*)
Does it always blow like this on your campus?

A photographer and a reporter, led by a lion-haired faculty member, are seen approaching across the wind-rippled lawn.

FACULTY MEMBER   Mr. Quilty, the town paper would like a picture of you.

REPORTER   How long will you be staying in Beardsley?

QUILTY   Oh, I don't know. A week. Perhaps longer.

REPORTER   You're on your way from the East to Arizona. Correct?

QUILTY   Yes. I share a ranch there with a few merry companions.

REPORTER   You are lecturing here on the Love of Art. How do you define "Art"?

Front of Humbert's Rented House
in Thayer Street, Beardsley. It is a two-story brick-and-stucco

affair, with an unkempt dandelion-invaded lawn which is in striking contrast to the adjacent neat garden of Miss Fenton Lebone, whose name is on the mailbox. She is inspecting the progress of certain bulbs when Humbert drives up. As he walks past her along the gravel path to his porch, the sound track registers his rapid mental supplication: Don't let Lebone notice me, don't have Miss Fenton Lebone talk to me, please don't let——. But the old lady's hawk eye has followed her neighbor's passage, and now she greets him sternly from behind her frontier of lilacs and laurels.

MISS LEBONE   Good afternoon, Professor.

HUMBERT   Oh. Hallo. (*Attempts to reach the safety of his door, but she will not be shaken off.*)

MISS LEBONE   I hate to intrude but don't you think you should do something about that jungle (*denouncing the dandelions*).

HUMBERT   (*trying a feeble quip*) Kindness to flowers. They are immigrants. We all are in a sense.

LEBONE   I'm certainly not. Couldn't I lend you my mower?

HUMBERT   Yes. Thanks. Perhaps Sunday.

LEBONE   You look exhausted.

HUMBERT   Yes, lots of work.

LEBONE   Incidentally, are you sure your pretty little girl gets enough sleep? I notice the light in her bedroom off and on, off and on, at all hours of the night.

[148]

That *is* her bedroom window, isn't it? There's a string
dangling from your pocket.

HUMBERT   Oh, thank you. Every time I undo a parcel
I put the string in my pocket. So stupid.

LEBONE   Now tell me—why doesn't your Dolly come
over to my house, any time, and curl up in a comfortable chair, and look at the *loads* of beautiful books
my dear mother gave me when *I* was a child. Wouldn't
that be much more wholesome than having the radio
at full blast for hours on end?

HUMBERT   Certainly. By all means. We'll do that.
(*He reaches the porch.*)

HUMBERT   (*mental monologue*) Should have said, as
we all are refugees in this world. Staircase wit. Abominable woman!

CUT TO:

The Humbert Home
There is a depressing atmosphere of disorder and neglect in
every room of the house.

HUMBERT   (*calling*) Lo! Lolita! Not in.

Leaning against the hallway telephone there is an empty Cola
bottle with its straw. In the living room, a stool is askew,
pushed away from the easy chair with a medley of magazines
spilled on the floor; a plate with crumbs stands on the TV;
a heap of bluebooks (ruins of a college examination)
have been left by Humbert on and around the divan. On a
small table there are the implements from Lolita's manicure

[149]

set: a bottle of nail polish has stuck to the varnished top of the table where it leaves a bald spot when removed; one ballet shoe sits on the piano, its mate lies sole up on the threshold to the next room. In the kitchen there is a mountain of dirty dishes in the sink; bottle caps strew the table where flies stroll around a chicken drumstick.

CUT TO:

Hallway—Lolita with her school chum, Mona Dahl
(a smartly dressed, experienced-looking, cool brunette), and two boys come in and troop into the living room, where with magic instantaneousness, as if awaiting them, music starts mewing and moaning. Humbert comes out on the upper landing from his study.

HUMBERT   (*calling down*) Lolita? Who's that?

LOLITA   (*climbing the stairs*) It's me, and Mona, and Roy, and Rex.

HUMBERT   Where have you been?

LOLITA   Oh, at the candy bar. And now I've come to fetch my sweater and swimsuit.

HUMBERT   What for?

LOLITA   (*pulling on the sweater, which she finds on the banister*) We are going to the BB River Club.

HUMBERT   The *what?*

LOLITA   (*laughing as she emerges Bardotesquely disheveled through the neckhole*) The Beach and Boat Club. Roy's father's a member.

[150]

HUMBERT   Now, first of all I don't want that racket in the living room. And in the second place, it's much too windy on the river today.

LOLITA   Oh, maybe we'll just hang around——

HUMBERT   Besides, my pet, the theme of boating has not been a particularly fortunate one in your young life.

LOLITA   Okay, okay, there are other things we can do there——

HUMBERT   You are not going.

LOLITA   They have a bowling alley and table tennis——

HUMBERT   You have your homework to do. And housework!

LOLITA   Jees——

HUMBERT   You tell your friends you're not going.

LOLITA   I'll do nothing of the sort.

HUMBERT   Then I will.

He clears his throat and descends the stairs. From the landing Lolita sees him entering the living room. The music stops, stunned. Swearing under her breath, Lolita runs down the steps toward her friends, as they are herded into the hallway from the living room by Humbert, whose constrained nervous smile and jaunty manner cannot mask his awkward boorishness.

MONA   Really, sir, we would not stop long out there.

HUMBERT   No-no-no.

ROY   I'm sure, sir, you have nothing to worry about.

HUMBERT   I'm sorry, children, but it will be some other time.

He dismisses them and ascends the staircase repeating that rasping sound in his throat. In the hallway, Lolita talks to her friends as they file out into the sun.

LOLITA   Well, you see—this is the way it is.

MONA   I'll call you later, Dolly. I think your sweater's dreamy.

LOLITA   Thank you. It's virgin wool.

MONA   The only thing about you that is, kiddo.

Mona's husky laugh recedes as Lolita closes the door after her. Humbert from the stairs has heard that exchange. Lolita runs up past him to her room. She fumbles for the key to lock herself in. Humbert, rumbling, follows her.

CUT TO:

Lolita's Very Untidy Bedroom

HUMBERT   I've removed that key long ago, my dear. There is no place in the world where you could——

LOLITA   You get out!

[152]

HUMBERT   *You* have no reason to be mad at *me*. Yes,
    I shall leave you to your meditations, but first I want
    to say something about that girl, Mona.

LOLITA   You can't have her. She belongs to a marine.

HUMBERT   I shall ignore that idiotic remark. What
    I mean to say is—can it possibly be that you have
    betrayed me to her?

LOLITA   Very melodramatic.
                            (*Clowns.*)
    You make me sick.
                            (*in a quieter smaller
                            voice*)
    Why can't I have fun with my friends?

HUMBERT   Because, Lolita, whenever you leave me,
    whenever you go somewhere without me, I start imagin-
    ing all sorts of things.

LOLITA   So I never can have *any* fun?

HUMBERT   But you do have fun. You asked for a
    bicycle—I gave you one. You wanted music lessons—
    I got you Miss Emperor, I mean, Miss King, who is
    the best pianist in town.

LOLITA   I want to act in the school play.

HUMBERT   My darling, we went into that before.
    Can't you see, the more exposed you are to contacts, to
    people, the more dangerous it all becomes. You and I
    have to guard our secret constantly. You say you want
    to act in a play. You *are* in a play as it is. In a very

difficult play where you have the part of an innocent schoolgirl. Stick to that role. It's quite big enough for one little performer.

LOLITA   Some day . . . Some day you'll be sorry.

HUMBERT   I know it's all very simple really. You don't love me. You never loved me. Isn't that the main problem?

LOLITA   Will you let me act in the play?

HUMBERT   Do you love me just a little, Lolita?

She looks at him, mysterious and meretricious, pondering whether to get what she wants by granting or by refusing.

CUT TO:

Living Room
Lolita is rehearsing. Mimeos of her part litter the furniture. From the kitchen threshold, Humbert tenderly observes her. She, like a hypnotic subject or a performer in a mystic rite, touches mirages of make-believe objects with her sly, slender, girl-child hands.

LOLITA   (*in romantic monotone*) Sleep, hunter. Velvet petals flutter down upon you. In this bower you will recline.

She gestures toward an invisible partner—and then, with a more normal movement, forehead puckered, searches for the rest of her part on a mimeographed sheet.

HUMBERT   (*gently*) If you have finished, come and have something to eat.

LOLITA   (*continuing her incantations*) I'll recite to you,
    hunter, a lullaby song about the mourning dove you lost
    when you were young. Listen!

> *Gone is Livia, love is gone:*
> *Strong wing, soft breast, bluish plume;*
> *In the juniper tree moaning at dawn:*
>   *doom, doom.*

HUMBERT   What an ominous last line. A perfect spon-
    dee but how depressing.

LOLITA   Lay off, will you? And now sleep, hunter,
    sleep. Under the raining rose petals, sleep, hunter.
        (*to Humbert*)
    What do you want?

HUMBERT   A five-minute pause. I want you to forget
    Mr. Hunter whoever he is.

She goes on with her tactile make-believe, stroking the air
before her with kneading fingers.

HUMBERT   What are you doing? Plucking a fruit?

LOLITA   Look—what does it matter to you?

HUMBERT   One would like to know.

LOLITA   Suppose I'm stroking the horn of my pet
    unicorn—what the heck is it to you?

HUMBERT   Okay, Hecuba.

LOLITA   Will you go, please? I'll come in a minute.

He looks at her with dewy eyes, in an ecstasy of tenderness and adoration. She, exasperated, bangs her fist on the piano keys and falls into an easy chair, her legs sideways over the armrest.

LOLITA   You will never leave me alone, is that it?

He goes down on his knees literally crawling toward her, adumbrating an amphoric embrace, almost like a lover of yore.

LOLITA   Oh, no! Not again.

HUMBERT   My love, my mourning dove! I'm so miserable! There is something gathering around us which I cannot understand. You are not telling me all, you——

Doorbell

LOLITA   Get up! Get up from the floor! It's Mona. I quite forgot. Let her in. I'll be down in a sec.

She rushes through the kitchen, picking up the wedge of pizza on the way, and runs upstairs to her room. From the upper landing she cries down to Mona, whom Humbert has let in:

LOLITA   I'm changing and coming down!

CUT TO:

Living Room
Mona saunters in, followed by Humbert.

HUMBERT   Are you going to rehearse? She's been at it all day.

[156]

MONA   Well, no. I'm driving Dolly to her piano
lesson.

HUMBERT   But today's Saturday? I thought Miss Emperor had changed the hour to Monday afternoon.

MONA   It's been changed back again.
(picking up a book)
Is this novel as good as some people say?

HUMBERT   Oh, I don't know. It's just an old love
story with a new twist. Superb artist, of course, but
who cares? We live in an age when the serious middle-
brow idiot craves for a literature of ideas, for the novel
of social comment.

MONA   I wish I could attend your lectures at Beardsley
College, sir. We young people of today are so much
in need of spiritual guidance.

HUMBERT   Tell me, young person of today, how was
that party at your aunt's the other night?

MONA   Oh, it was sweet of you to allow Dolly to come.

HUMBERT   So the party was a success?

MONA   Oh, a riot, terrific.

HUMBERT   Did Dolly, as you call her, dance a lot?

MONA   Not a frightful lot. Why?

HUMBERT   I suppose all the boys are mad about her?

MONA   Well, sir, the fact is Dolly isn't much concerned with mere boys. They bore her.

HUMBERT   What about that Roy what's-his-name?

MONA   Oh, him.

A languorous shrug.

HUMBERT   What do you think of Dolly?

MONA   Oh, she's a swell kid.

HUMBERT   Is she very frank with you?

MONA   Oh, she's a doll.

HUMBERT   I mean, I suppose you and she——

Lolita runs into the room.

MONA   Dolly, your piano lesson is today. Remember? Not Monday. I came to fetch you as we agreed. Remember?

HUMBERT   Eight o'clock punctually, Lolita.

The two girls leave.

CUT TO:

The School Auditorium
A gauze curtain has just come down and the young performers are taking a last bow. Quilty's pudgy hands are briefly seen meatily clapping, as Lolita dreamily smiles across

the footlights. Vivian Darkbloom, darkly blooming, blows her a kiss. The applause gradually subsides.

CUT TO:

Backstage
An atmosphere of exuberant success. Miss King, the piano teacher, greets tuxedo-clad Humbert.

HUMBERT   Glad to see you, Miss Emperor.

MISS KING   King.

HUMBERT   Yes, of course. Miss King. A thousand excuses. I keep thinking of the piano teacher in *Madame Bovary*. Well, I must thank you for giving Lolita so much time.

MISS KING   So much time? Why, on the contrary, she seems to have been much too busy with rehearsals. Let me see: she must have missed at least four lessons.

Lolita emerges from the greenroom. She is glamorous. She is excited. She has not yet shed her wings.

LOLITA   (*to Humbert*) You can go home now. Mona is taking me to her aunt's place for refreshments.

HUMBERT   You're coming with me. Home. At once.

LOLITA   I've promised Mona. Oh, please!

HUMBERT   No.

LOLITA   I'll do anything if you let me go.

HUMBERT   No.

LOLITA   I love you.

HUMBERT   Love me? With that lethal hate in those
    painted eyes? No, my girl, you'll come home and prac-
    tice the piano.

He grasps her by the hand. A struggle would be indecorous.
Exeunt.

CUT TO:

Car
It pulls up. Humbert and Lolita come out in front of their
house. Lolita attempts to move away.

HUMBERT   Where are you going? Come here.

LOLITA   I want to ride my bike. I need some fresh air,
    you brute.

HUMBERT   You're coming in with me.

LOLITA   For Christ's sake——

CUT TO:

Hallway

HUMBERT   I know you are unfaithful to me. There's a
    tangled web around me. But I will not surrender. You
    cannot torment me like that. I have a right to know, I
    have a right to struggle.

[160]

LOLITA   Finished?

HUMBERT   And that's all you can answer?

LOLITA   If you've finished, I'll get something to eat. You
cheated me out of a luscious supper.

CUT TO:

The Kitchen
Lolita has finished her sandwich and is messily fishing out
slippery peach halves from a can. Humbert, throbbing with
rage, makes himself a drink. She eats, reading a comic book
and scratching her calf.

HUMBERT   What a fool—what a fool, this Humbert!
Giving little Lolita numberless humbertless opportuni-
ties! Dreamy bicycle rides, sunsets, lovers' lanes, piano
lessons, rehearsals, ditches, garages, coal sheds.

Lolita, having finished her meal, walks to the door.

CUT TO:

Living Room
Lolita sprawling in an overstuffed chair. She bites at a hang-
nail and mocks Humbert with her heartless eyes. She has
placed one outstretched shoeless foot in coarse white sock on
a stool which she rocks with heel and toe.

LOLITA   Well, speak, lover.

Humbert paces the room rubbing his cheek with his fist in a
tremor of exasperation.

[161]

LOLITA   Because, if you don't want to speak to me, in
    a couple of minutes, I'll go riding my bicycle.

Humbert sinks down in a chair facing her. She continues to
stare at him and to rock the stool.

HUMBERT   I doubt you'll be using your bicycle much
    longer now.

LOLITA   Oh, yah?

He controls himself and tries to speak calmly but in the course
of his speech his voice gradually rises to a hysterical pitch.
And the window is open with the lilacs listening.

HUMBERT   Dolores, this must stop right away. You are
    ruining our relationship and jeopardizing your own
    safety. I don't know, nor wish to know, what young
    hoodlum, Roy or Foy, you are dating in secret. But all
    this must stop or else anything may happen.

LOLITA   Anything may happen, huh?

He snatches away the stool she is toe-heel rocking, and her
foot falls with a thud.

LOLITA   Hey, take it easy!

Humbert grabs her by her thin wrist as she attempts to run
out of the room.

HUMBERT   No, you'll listen to me! I'll break your
    wrist, but you'll listen. Tomorrow—yes tomorrow—
    we'll leave, we'll go to Mexico, we'll start a completely
    new life.

She manages to twist out of his grip and runs out of the house.

Humbert rushes out into the street and sees her pedaling townward. With one hand pressed to his palpitating heart, he makes for the corner, and then continues to the familiar drugstore. In the lamplight her bicycle, self-conscious and demure, is leaning against a post. Humbert enters the drugstore. At its far end, Lolita is revealed through the glass of a telephone booth, a little mermaid in a tank. She is still speaking. To whom? Me? Cupping the tube, confidentially hunched over it, she slits her eyes at Humbert, hangs up, and walks out of the booth.

LOLITA   (*brightly*) Tried to reach you at home.

HUMBERT   You did? That's odd. I saw you speaking, I saw your lips move.

LOLITA   Yes, I got the wrong number. Look, I don't want you to be mad at me any more. Everything is going to be all right from now on. I've reached a great decision.

HUMBERT   Oh, Lolita. If only I could still believe you.

She smiles at him and straddles her bike.

Thayer Street, leading home
A glistening night. Along the damp pavement Lolita half-rides her bike, pushing against the curb with one foot, waiting for Humbert to catch up, and then propelling herself again. He walks behind, agitated, moist-eyed, jerkily trying to keep up with her. A dog strains on its leash, and its owner allows it to sniff at a lamppost. The CAMERA follows Humbert and

Lolita as they approach the house. Lilacs in bloom. The neighbor's lighted window goes out.

CUT TO:

Hallway. Lolita and Humbert enter

LOLITA   Carry me upstairs. I feel kind of romantic tonight.

He gathers her up. The telephone rings.

LOLITA   (*raising her index finger*) Telephone.

HUMBERT   Oh, let it ring!

LOLITA   Put me down, put me down. Never disappoint a telephone.

HUMBERT   My aphoristic darling! All right.

On the telephone Quilty speaks in a disguised muffled croak-voice.

QUILTY   How are you, Prof?

HUMBERT   Fine. May I——

QUILTY   Sorry to disturb you at such a late hour. Are you enjoying your stay at Beardsley?

HUMBERT   Yes. May I inquire who's calling?

QUILTY   This is the best time of the year but we might do with some rain.

[164]

HUMBERT   Sorry—who's calling?

QUILTY   (*with a pleasant laugh*) We haven't actually met but I've been keeping a friendly eye on you. Could I talk to you on the phone for a minute?

HUMBERT   Are you connected with the college?

QUILTY   In a way. I am a kind of extramural student. You see, I am studying your case.

HUMBERT   What case? I don't understand.

QUILTY   Is Dolores in bed?

HUMBERT   Oh, that's what it is. Are you disguising your voice, Roy Walker?

QUILTY   No, no. You are mistaken.

HUMBERT   Well, all I can tell you is that neither she nor I welcomes calls from strangers.

QUILTY   (*very suavely*) This is a complete misunderstanding. The group I represent is merely anxious that children should not keep late hours. You see, Mr. Humbert, I am a private member of the Public Welfare Board.

HUMBERT   What's your name?

QUILTY   Oh, it's an obscure unremarkable name. My department, sir, wants to check some bizarre rumors concerning the relationship between you and that pretty child. We have certain plans for her. We know an elderly gentleman, a bachelor of independent means, who would be eager to adopt her.

In the course of this speech Humbert takes a pillbox out of his waistcoat and swallows a tablet.

HUMBERT   This is ridiculous.

QUILTY   Have you adopted her? Legally, I mean?

HUMBERT   Well, I——

QUILTY   Have you filed a petition? Your stutter proclaims you have not.

HUMBERT   I assume that a stepfather is a relative and that a relative is a natural guardian.

QUILTY   Are you aware that the word "natural" has rather sinister connotations?

HUMBERT   Not in my case, no.

QUILTY   But you agree that a minor female must have a guardian?

HUMBERT   I suppose so.

QUILTY   And that she is not merely a pet?

HUMBERT   I really——

QUILTY   You moved here from Ramsdale, Professor?

HUMBERT   That's right. But——

In the meantime Lolita has crept into the hallway and enlaced Humbert with her bare arm.

QUILTY   Are you aware that some states prohibit a guardian from changing the ward's residence without an order of the court?

HUMBERT   Which states?

QUILTY   For example, the state you are in: a state of morbid excitement. Have you seen your psychiatrist lately?

HUMBERT   I neither have nor need one.

QUILTY   You are classified in our files as a white widowed male. Are you prepared to give our investigator a report on your present sex life, if any?

HUMBERT   Investigator?

Humbert nervously strokes caressive Lolita's wrist.

QUILTY   Yes. We intend our Dr. Blanche Schwarzman, a very efficient lady, to visit you at your convenience.

HUMBERT   I'm afraid I have nothing to tell her.

QUILTY   "Afraid" is Freudian lingo.

HUMBERT   I do not follow you. Give me your address and I shall write you.

QUILTY   That's unnecessary. After tomorrow our doctor will examine you and your protégée. I now hang up.

Living Room
Humbert walking about nervously.

HUMBERT   It's a hoax. It's a hoax. But that's immaterial. Rumors, he said. Oh, *mon Dieu!*

LOLITA   We must go away.

HUMBERT   We must flee as in an old melodrama. Our safest bet is to go abroad.

LOLITA   Okay—let's go to Mexico. I was conceived there.

HUMBERT   I'm sure I'll find a lecturing job there. Marvelous! I know a Spanish poet in Mexico City. He is full of black bulls and symbols, and as corny as a matador. But he is influential.

LOLITA   One condition. This time *I* am going to trace out our route. I want to take in Arizona. I want to see the Indian dances in Elphinstone.

HUMBERT   (*weeping*) I'm in your hands, your hot little hands, my love.

It is assumed that from Beardsley (which is situated in Idaho) to the Mexican border (via Arizona) the distance is at least 1,000 miles. Our fugitives start Wednesday morning. Humbert, who is eager to reach with the least delay Borderton, S. Arizona (and thence, Mexico's West Coast Highway) intends to be there Friday morning. In a naive effort to be inconspicuous he plans to sleep two nights in the car (the first, within the parking area of a trailer court and the second, somewhere in the Arizona desert). It is further assumed that Quilty, using three or four different rented cars, so as to avoid identification and confuse his victim, pursues Humbert from Idaho, through Nevada (or Utah), to Arizona. Quilty's plan is to have Humbert transport the minor female across two state lines down to Elphinestone, Arizona, where he will kidnap her and take her to his ranch in that vicinity. During the journey, there arises the problem how to get Lolita's luggage out of the car. This is attempted at the stop in Waco, Thursday morning (and successfully brought off on the following Monday, with the unplanned help of Lolita's hospitalization). The glimpses Humbert has had of Quilty before (e.g., in Briceland and Beardsley) had been too casual and brief to allow recognition. Quilty takes care to remain a fleet shadow, a ghostly predator, as he keeps up with Humbert on the road, now overtaking him, now awaiting his passage. Humbert's anxiety and rage are increased by his not quite knowing if it is a sleuth or a suitor.

CUT TO:

Humbert's Eyes in the Rearview Mirror
He and Lolita are driving along a canyon into the small burg of Cottonwood: three poplars and alfalfa fields.

LOLITA   We'll crash into something if you keep looking
back.

HUMBERT   What a bizarre situation!

LOLITA   You're telling me. I've been riding with a nut
all day.

HUMBERT   —bizarre because there's no general way of dealing with this kind of case. That car has been following us, on and off, for the last two hundred miles. I can't very well complain to the highway patrol.

LOLITA   (*laughing*) You certainly can't!

HUMBERT   But I can try to give him the slip.

LOLITA   Not with this jalopy.

HUMBERT   (*going through a changing light in Cottonwood*) Ah, the red light will stop him.

LOLITA   You'll get arrested if you do that.

HUMBERT   And here we'll turn and hide for a minute. In this nice little lane.

LOLITA   It's a one-way little lane.

HUMBERT   True.

He backs out.

LOLITA   Besides it's illegal to play games with other cars on the road.

HUMBERT   Will you stop chattering. I almost hit that van.

LOLITA   Look. Let's get back to the highway and just ignore the whole business.

CUT TO:

[170]

*The Highway Again—evening of the same day—low blinding
sun*
Lolita is eating a banana in the moving car.

CUT TO:

Service Station
Needing a pair of new sunglasses, Humbert leaves Lolita in
the car and walks into the office of the station. His pursuer
quietly pulls up just across the street while Humbert is select-
ing the glasses. He glances through a side window.

CUT TO:

Humbert's Car
Quilty has walked up to it and Lolita is leaning out and talking to him rapidly, her hand with outspread fingers going up
and down, as it does when she is very serious and emphatic.
Humbert is struck by the voluble familiarity of her manner.
The conversation is not heard (except, perhaps, for the word
"Elphinstone"), and Quilty's face is not seen. He bolts back
to his convertible, which disappears as Humbert comes out of
the office.

CUT TO:

Humbert's Car moving up a steep grade

HUMBERT   What did that man ask you, Lo?

LOLITA   (*studying a road map*) Man? Oh, that man.
    Oh, yes. Oh, I don't know. He wondered if I had a map.
    Lost his way, I guess.

A pause.

HUMBERT   Now listen, Lo. I don't know if you are lying or not. I don't know if you are insane or not—but that person has been following us all day, and I think he is a cop.

LOLITA   (*laughing*) If he's really a cop the worst thing we could do would be to show that we are scared. Oh, look: all the nines are changing into the next thousand. When I was a little kid I used to think they'd stop and go back to nines if only my mother would agree to back the car.

CUT TO:

Market

HUMBERT   Let me see—we wanted——

He broods among the fruit, a rotting Priap, listening to a melon, questioning a peach, pushing his wire cart toward the lacquered strawberries. Lolita has been loitering near the window where the magazine rack is. She sees Quilty haunting the sidewalk. Satisfying herself that Humbert is engrossed in his shopping, she slips out. Presently, burdened with his cornucopian paper bag, Humbert comes out of the store looking around for Lolita. He leaves the bag in the parked car, locks it again, and then paces the sidewalk peering into various shops as he proceeds along a series of Drugs, Real Estate, Auto Parts, Café, Sporting Goods, Real Estate, Furniture, Drugs, Western Union, Cleaners, Appliances, Betty's Beauty Parlor. As he walks back, in pain and panic, he suddenly descries her trying to retrieve her new coat and traveling case out of the car; but the doors are locked, and she can't pull out her things through the three-quarters closed window (Quilty the shadow is ambushed in a side street, the idea

being that she join him with some of her treasured posses-
sions). She notices Humbert approaching—and, slitting her
eyes, walks toward him with feigned nonchalance.

LOLITA   Oh, there you are.

For a few seconds Humbert looks at her in grim silence.

LOLITA   What's the matter?

HUMBERT   You were gone twenty minutes. I cannot
    tolerate these vanishing acts. I want to know exactly
    where you've been—and with whom.

LOLITA   I ran into a girl friend.

HUMBERT   Really?

LOLITA   You calling me a liar?

HUMBERT   Her name, please.

LOLITA   Oh, just a kid I went to school with.

HUMBERT   Beardsley School?

LOLITA   Yes. Oh, yes. Beardsley.

HUMBERT   Her name?

LOLITA   Betty. Betty Parker.

HUMBERT   Perfect. Here, in this little black book,
    Volume 2, I have a list of your schoolmates. Let's see.
    Hm. There's a Mary Paddington, and a Julia Pierce.
    But no Parker. What say you?

LOLITA   She was not in my group.

HUMBERT   That's the entire school I have listed here.

LOLITA   She enrolled just before we left.

HUMBERT   Well, let's try another angle. Where exactly did you meet her?

LOLITA   Oh, I saw her from the grocery. She was just loafing around like me.

HUMBERT   And what did you do next?

LOLITA   We went to a drugstore.

HUMBERT   And you had there——?

LOLITA   Couple of Cokes.

HUMBERT   Careful, my girl. We can check that, you know.

LOLITA   At least, she had. I had a glass of water.

HUMBERT   The anonymous fluid. I see. Very good. Was it that place over there?

LOLITA   Sure.

HUMBERT   Good. Come on, we'll grill the soda jerk.

LOLITA   Wait a sec. Come to think, it might have been the other store, on the corner.

HUMBERT   Confrontation delayed. But it's all right. We'll try both.

LOLITA   Or perhaps in one of the side streets.

HUMBERT   We'll find it. Here, let's go into this telephone booth. You rather like telephone booths, don't you? Now, let's consult the directory. This dirty book. This chained and battered book. Dignified Funeral Service. No, we don't need that yet. Here we are. Druggists, Retail. Hill Drug Store. Corner Drug Store. Cypress Lane Drugs. And Larkin's Pharmacy. Well, that's all they have around here. And we'll check them one by one.

LOLITA   Go to hell.

HUMBERT   My dear, rudeness will get you nowhere.

LOLITA   You are not going to trap me. Okay. So we didn't have a pop. We just talked and walked, and looked at dresses in show windows.

HUMBERT   That window, for example?

LOLITA   Yes, that window for example.

HUMBERT   Oh, Lolita! Let us look closer at it.

CUT TO:

The Show Window of a dress store.
A man, on his hands and knees, is rearranging the carpet on which a wedding group stands in a more or less dismantled state ("as if a blast had just worked havoc with them"): one

wigless and armless figure is naked except for white spats. Another, a sexless little nude, stands in a smirking pose, with a
posy, and would represent, when clothed, a flower girl of
Lolita's size. The taller, lavishly veiled bride is complete but
lacks one arm. On the floor, where the employee crawls, there
lies a cluster of three bare arms and a blond wig. Two of the
arms, not necessarily a pair, happen to be twisted and seem to
suggest a clasping gesture of horror and supplication. Humbert, tense and bitter, his face twitching, points out these details to sullen Lolita.

HUMBERT   Look, Lolita. Look well. Isn't this a grue-
    some symbol of something or other? Doesn't it make
    your delicate flesh creep a little?

CUT TO:

*A Highway, low sun, Shadow of Car running and fluctuating
on a rock bank—a Sign:*
    ELPHINSTONE 20 M.
Lolita is ill. She covers her eyes with her hand, throws her
head back, moans.

HUMBERT   Tired?

She does not respond.

HUMBERT   Would you like me to stop? You might nap
    for an hour or two.

She shrugs her shoulders.

HUMBERT   Don't you feel well?

LOLITA   I feel utterly rotten.

[176]

HUMBERT   Why, what's the matter, my darling? Tummy?

LOLITA   Everything. I want to stop at Elphinstone for the night.

HUMBERT   Oh, but we'll never make Borderton at this rate.

LOLITA   I'm dying, you dope. We'll spend the night in Elphinstone.

HUMBERT   I wanted to avoid motels.

LOLITA   Well, this time we'll go to the best one in Elphinstone. I underlined it in the AAA book. Dream Hacienda. Oh, I've never felt so awful in all my life! You're sitting on my sweater.

HUMBERT   My poor darling! What a setback. Tsk-tsk. I know what we'll do. At the next turnout I'll take your temperature. I have a thermometer in my overnight bag.

CUT TO:

Turnout—a sheer cliff rising on the far side of the highway and a misty abyss melting just beyond the rim of the turnout Lolita, her head on the nape rest, eyes closed, endures the thermometer stuck in her mouth. The CAMERA gingerly inspects the litter receptacles with their cans and containers, and a small child's sneaker forgotten on the stone parapet. Humbert consulting his wristwatch.

HUMBERT   Well, I think we can peep now.

Tenderly he removes the glass tube from her mouth. She licks her parched lips and shivers. Humbert tries to make out the level of the mercury.

HUMBERT   These tricky American thermometers are meant to conceal their information from the layman. Ah, here we are. Good God, one hundred and three. I must take you straight to a hospital.

Quilty has pulled up at the next turnout.

CUT TO:

Dream Hacienda Motel at Elphinstone, Arizona—a fine morning
Humbert is seen coming out of his unit with several books under his arm and a bunch of rather straggly wild flowers. The landlady talks to him as he goes to his car.

LANDLADY   I hope she's much better today.

HUMBERT   Well, I'm driving over to see. The doctor said that in this kind of flu there's a distinct drop in temperature on the fourth day, and indeed she had hardly any fever yesterday.

LANDLADY   She'll love the flowers.

HUMBERT   I picked them in the ravine at the back of your place. Cold breeze today. Is it the elevation?

LANDLADY   Oh, it's hot enough for me.

HUMBERT   I'm not feeling well. Guess I'll lie down when I return.

LANDLADY   Wait a minute. I'll remove this basket of
    linen so you can turn more easily.

CUT TO:

A Sunny Private Room in the Elphinstone Hospital
Lolita, looking happy and innocent, lies in her neat bed with
a magazine, her lips freshly painted, her hair brilliantly
brushed. There is a white telephone, a topaz ring, and one rose
in a glass with bubble-gemmed stem on the bedside table.
Mary Lore, a plump, comely, arrogant young nurse who is in
cahoots with the nymphet, is folding very rapidly a white
flannel blanket as Humbert enters with his pathetic bouquet
and books.

HUMBERT   *Bonjour, mon petit.*

LOLITA   What gruesome funeral flowers. Thanks all the
    same. But do you mind cutting out the French, it annoys
    everybody.

Her eyes go back to her magazine.

HUMBERT   Temperature normal? Well, that's splendid.
    Who gave you that rose?

LOLITA   Mary.

MARY LORE   (*glancing window-ward at the yard be-
    low*) You can't park there, Mister. You have to go
    around to the other end.

HUMBERT   Sorry. I was in a hurry—and I don't feel
    too well.

[179]

MARY   There is a sign saying "staff only."

HUMBERT   All right, all right.

Exit Mary with blanket.

LOLITA   Mary was trying to be helpful.

HUMBERT   Mary is arrogant and nosy. I would not
wonder, my dear, if you two had swapped every kind
of crummy confession. That rump of hers must make
interns pant.

LOLITA   Your English is showing vahst improvement,
my deah. You'll be using delinquent lingo next.

A pause.

HUMBERT   I brought you some rather fascinating
books: *The History of Dancing. The Romantic Poets* by
my friend Professor Behr. *Flowers of the Rockies,* with
excellent illustrations. And *Carmen* by Mérimée—not a
very good translation, I'm afraid, but do read it, it's a
marvelous melancholy story.

Lolita emits a grunt of indifferent gratitude and continues to
consume her magazine. Mary Lore bustles in again.

HUMBERT   (*picking up a pair of sunglasses from the
top of a chest of drawers*) Oh—whose are these? Not
mine, not yours.

MARY   (*after exchanging a quick glance with Lolita*)
Then it's a visitor left them.

HUMBERT   Visitor? You had a visitor, Lolita?

MARY   (*pocketing the glasses*) Another patient had. I found them in the corridor and thought they might be yours.

HUMBERT   *Est-ce que tu ne m'aimes plus, ma Carmen?* My Carmen does not love me any more?

LOLITA   There we go again.

She flips through her magazine, finds the continuation, and reads on.

HUMBERT   The thermometer broke in the glove compartment but I took my pulse this morning and it was one hundred and ten. I shall soon leave you and go to bed. Don't you want to look at the nice books I brought you?

Lolita emits again her neutral grunt and picks her nose as she plunges deeper into "They called me a Harlot." Humbert lowers himself into a cretonne chair, opens the botanical work he has brought her, and attempts to identify his flowers. This proves impossible.

HUMBERT   (*with a sigh*) I'll be going away in a minute. I'm not feeling well at all. Don't you want to talk to me?

LOLITA   What?

HUMBERT   I said don't you want to talk to me? You'll read your magazine when I'm gone.

LOLITA   What do you want me to tell you?

Mary Lore reenters with a vase for the flowers.

HUMBERT   I'm wondering if you should not leave the
hospital tomorrow. You look the image of radiant
health.

MARY   She will stay till Tuesday. Doctor's orders. Horse
mint, poison oak. And this goldenrod will give her hay
fever.

HUMBERT   Oh, throw them out, throw them out.

MARY   Yes, I think I had better remove them.

She exits.

HUMBERT   Lolita! My love! Just think—Tuesday if
we start early we'll be in Mexico by noon. No mysterious
agents, no ghosts, no ghouls will follow us any longer.
We shall be free to live as we like, my Lolita. I'll make
you a formal proposal. An old priest will bless us, and
we shall live happily forever after, in lovely Rosa-
morada.

Both realize that Mary Lore is again in the room.

LOLITA   He's reciting poetry. Don't mind him, Mary.

HUMBERT   Yes, poetry. The only reality on this earth.
Well, I'll be on my way.

LOLITA   I want all my things. The brown bag, mother's
blue one, the car sack, everything.

HUMBERT   They are still in the car. I did not take them
   to the motel.

LOLITA   Well, I want them right now.

HUMBERT   Couldn't you wait till Tuesday? I mean,
   you don't want *all* your frocks immediately.

LOLITA   That's for me to decide. Where's that hand
   mirror, Mary?

HUMBERT   I don't feel strong enough to carry all that
   luggage.

MARY   Oh, we'll have Joe do it, don't you worry.

HUMBERT   All right. I think I'll go now. Well, good-
   bye, Lolita.

LOLITA   (*looking at herself in the hand mirror*) Bye-
   bye.

HUMBERT   Girl with a Hand Glass. Artist unknown.

He considers her, softly swinging the car keys he holds. Mary
waits at the door.

CUT TO:

Motel Room
Humbert is asleep asprawl on one of the twin beds. He is in
the throes of a virus infection and has been drinking freely
from the bottle of gin beside him. The bedside telephone rings.
It takes him some time to come out of his sick slumber.

VOICE   Hi there, Professor.

HUMBERT   Who's calling?

VOICE   Are you all right?

HUMBERT   Not exactly.

VOICE   Not feeling too good, eh?

HUMBERT   No. Who is it?

VOICE   Not enjoying your trip? That's too bad.

HUMBERT   What d'you want?

VOICE   I'm not sure what to call it. Cooperation? Surrender to fate?

HUMBERT   All right. If you are not a hallucination, not a mere tinnitus——

VOICE   A *what?* .

HUMBERT   Tinnitus—a singing in the ears, because I have a high fever——

VOICE   Frankly, I'm also nursing some sort of bug. Guess, we both caught it from her.

HUMBERT   From her? What d'you mean?

VOICE   Oh, lots of things are feminine—cars, carpets, car pets, haha! I've even heard a fireman refer to a fire as she.

[184]

HUMBERT   If you're not my delirium——

VOICE   Skip it. Look, Bertie, I just wanted to make sure you're safe in bed. Good-nitus.

HUMBERT   If I'm not fancying things, then you must be the person who's been following me.

VOICE   Well, that's all finished now. You're not followed any more. I'll be leaving in a minute with my little niece. (Aside: You stay out of this.)

HUMBERT   Wait!

VOICE   Good-nitus, good-nitus. (*with a laugh*) I know exactly what you'll do as soon as I hang up.

He hangs up. Humbert frantically searches for the scrap of paper on which he has jotted down the telephone number connecting him with Lolita at the hospital. Finds it and dials. A nurse's voice answers, but is engulfed in Quilty's rich baritone.

VOICE   I'll take it. It's for me. Well, isn't that pat. I told you I knew you would do it. Sorry I can't talk now. She's in my lap and quite lively.

Hangs up guffawing.
Humbert is about to dial again—but thinks better of it and in a frenzy of horror and hurry pulls on some clothes and stumbles out.

CUT TO:

The Vestibule of Elphinstone Hospital—a spacious lobby with a staircase on either side and offices at the farther end.

There are several people around. Joking Joe, a robust male nurse, is in the act of wheeling a mummylike patient out of the elevator. Nurse Mary Lore is preening herself on the first landing. Doctor Blue is coming out of the x-ray department perusing a cloudy picture, the galaxy of a lung. Two old men in a corner are playing chess, and a third old-timer is inspecting the titles of several books (*Flowers of the Rockies,* etc.) heaped on a chair. As Humbert rushes in and launches into his dramatic, drunken, sick, hysterical expostulations, the various people around freeze in various positions.

HUMBERT   Lolita! Lolita! Lolita!

MARY LORE   (*tripping down the steps*) We don't want a scene——

HUMBERT   Where is she?

MARY   You know perfectly well that her uncle was to come for her today.

HUMBERT   I know nothing of the sort.

DR. BLUE   Take it easy. What's the matter, Mary?

MARY   He's sick and doesn't know what he's saying. The girl's uncle just took her away.

HUMBERT   It's a hellish conspiracy.

MARY   She warned me her stepfather had a feud with the rest of the family.

HUMBERT   A hellish lie! Where is she? I demand an answer.

[186]

DR. BLUE   Now, now, don't get excited.

Humbert tries to get hold of Mary Lore. He almost manages to clutch her. She gives a melodious yelp and twists free. The patient, who has been wheeled out by Joe, rises like Lazarus and joins Joe and Dr. Blue who are subduing Humbert.

CUT TO:

Psychiatrist
speaking (this is Dr. Ray who appears in the Prologue and will appear again at the very end of Act Three):

PSYCHIATRIST   As we now know from his notes, Humbert Humbert spent many a dismal month trying in vain to locate his lost Lolita and to establish the identity of her mysterious abductor. His quest merely resulted in impairing his health. At the sanatorium where he was treated for a heart condition, attention was also given to his mental state. The present speaker and two other psychiatrists endeavored to help Mr. Humbert but dissimulation had become second nature with him. My assistants and I tried to open channels of communication for the patient by providing a background of refinement and ease, soft music, amusing hobbies, and a permissive atmosphere in which he might dare express his most dangerous thoughts. However, the patient not only refused to indulge in voluptuous or vengeful fantasies, but insulted the therapist by calling him "the rapist of Psyche the Soul." He sneered at cooperation. He was abusive, he was taciturn. And Dr. Christina Fine, a lovely lady and a very strong analyst, complained that the patient kept trying to hypnotize her and make her divulge her innermost cravings. I am happy to say she is now my wife.

By the beginning of the following year, the patient's physical condition had improved so much that he was able to check out and join again the faculty of Beardsley College.

CUT TO:

A Neutral Place
The detective whom Humbert had hired to look for Lolita is reporting to him for the last time.

DETECTIVE   I'm afraid we'll have to give it up.

HUMBERT   Couldn't you go on? You said you would investigate the New Mexico clue.

DETECTIVE   Proved a dud. Dolores Hayes, H, A, Y, E, S, is a fat old dame selling homemade Tokay to the Indians.

HUMBERT   What about Canada?

DETECTIVE   What about the wide world? She might be a model in Brazil or a dancer in Paris.

HUMBERT   But isn't it merely a question of time? Can't *everybody* be tracked down finally?

DETECTIVE   Look, mister. We don't even have good pictures of her, she's just a kid in them. By now she may have three babies of her own.

HUMBERT   You are sure you could not keep trying?

DETECTIVE   It would just mean taking your money.

HUMBERT   I want the photos back.

DETECTIVE   We'll keep one or two in our files just in case. This one, in fancy dress, for instance.

He returns a number of photographs to Humbert. They should give a brief pictorial summary of Lolita's past life with him: Kneeling, half-naked, in a patch of sun on a mat; standing beside her mother on the dappled lawn; attending a school ball in full-skirted flamingo dress; in blue jeans and T-shirt, sprawling with a comic book; in dirty shorts, getting into a canoe (Charlie handing her a paddle from the bushy bank); in the passenger seat of Humbert's car; feeding a chipmunk; riding a pony; wearing black tights; in fancy dress on the stage.

CUT TO:

Beardsley College
Men and women students are seen streaming out into a courtyard. Humbert, with books and papers under his arm, walks to the parking lot. Mrs. Fowler, a lean, elegant, forty-year-old flirt, the wife of the Head of the Department, calls out to Humbert from inside her car.

MRS. FOWLER   Hullo, Humbert.

HUMBERT   Hullo, Diana.

MRS. FOWLER   Do you know if my husband is through with his seminar?

HUMBERT   Yes, I think I saw him going to his office.

MRS. FOWLER   He said he would finish a little earlier. We are to pick up a niece of mine at the airport. The poor kid lost her mother last year, and now her father has cancer.

HUMBERT   Oh.

MRS. FOWLER   I am so sorry for the child. We'll take her to the Riviera in spring. When is *your* sabbatical, Humbert?

HUMBERT   Alas, I've been here only two years.

He stands leaning with his elbows on the sill of her car. She puts her hand on his.

MRS. FOWLER   You must come to see us more often. Frank will be away on a lecture tour next month, and I will be very lonesome. Would you teach me chess? I think it's such a glamorous medieval game.

Frank Fowler comes up.

MRS. FOWLER   (*to her husband*) I was telling Humbert we must get together soon.

FOWLER   Yah. What about Sunday? Come have dinner with us.

CUT TO:

The Fowlers' Living Room
Bourgeois abstract art on the walls. They are having pre-prandial drinks with their guests. Frank Fowler gulps down the contents of a tall tumbler.

FOWLER   (*to Humbert*) Another Scotch? Well, I think I shall.

MRS. FOWLER   No, Frank, that's enough before dinner.

FOWLER   How does it feel to be a bachelor, Humbert? Must be a heavenly sensation.

HUMBERT   I was twice married.

MRS. FOWLER   Oh, were you?

HUMBERT   My second wife died four years ago. I inherited a stepdaughter.

MRS. FOWLER   But that's fascinating, Humbert. How old is she?

HUMBERT   Oh, she must be quite old by now. More than seventeen. She's living her own life somewhere. I've lost track of her.

A nymphet comes in.

MRS. FOWLER   This is Nina, my niece.

In the course of the following dialogue Humbert pays no attention to the child, and only at the last moment, as she turns away, and he sinks back into his chair with a tidbit picked from a remote plate, does he permit himself one brief, sad, ember-hot, tiger-quick glance.

MRS. FOWLER   When is Rosemary coming to fetch you?

NINA   I dunno. Soon, I guess.

MRS. FOWLER   What picture are you going to see?

NINA   Oh, some western. I don't care.

MRS. FOWLER   (*smiling*) Okay. Run along.

Nina indolently leaves.

MRS. FOWLER   She is twelve and in her blasé period, if you please.

FOWLER   I think I'll spank her if she perseveres in that droopy style.

MRS. FOWLER   Oh, she'll be all right after we take her to Europe.

FOWLER   What's your vacation going to be, Humbert, m'boy?

HUMBERT   I have no definite plans.

FOWLER   Come with us to Cap Topaz. It's the best spot on the Riviera.

HUMBERT   I know it well. My father owned a big hotel not far from there. The Mirana. It has degenerated now into an apartment house.

MRS. FOWLER   Will you come, Humbert? We'll gamble at the casino.

HUMBERT   I dare not gamble any more.

MRS. FOWLER   Well, Frank and I will, and you can sprawl on the *plage,* and build sand castles with Nina. Is that a deal? Will you come?

[192]

HUMBERT   What again? The old pang? The perilous
    magic? No. I'm not coming with you. The excitement
    would be too much. I have a weak heart, you know.

MAID   Dinner is served.

CUT TO:

An Exchange of Good Nights
on the lighted steps of the Fowler home. Humbert walks off.
His steps resound on the deserted sidewalk.

HUMBERT   I'm very lonely and I'm very drunk. The
    old magic. Kill Frank Fowler, marry Diana, drown
    Diana, inherit Nina, kill self. Oh, my Lolita, Lolita,
    Lolita. . . .

Next Day.

CUT TO:

Lecture Hall
Humbert has just finished his routine lecture and is collecting
his notes. A male student comes up to the lectern.

STUDENT   I've been auditing your lectures, Professor.
    My name is Shatzki, Norbert Shatzki, you had my sister
    in your class three years ago, she sends you her kindest
    regards.

HUMBERT   Oh yes. Yes.

SHATZKI   She's married now. I was wondering, sir, if
    you would also cover Edgar Poe's other loves?

In the meantime, another student, a girl, has entered the class-room.

GIRL   May I audit your lectures, Professor Humbert?

HUMBERT   (*absentmindedly, paying little attention to either of them, still collecting his notes*) If you like. No, I'll ignore his other romances.

GIRL   I'm taking philosophy, but I hope to enroll in your courses next year.

HUMBERT   Yes. Yes.

He is now ready to leave.

GIRL   I see you don't recognize me at all, at all, mon-sieur.

HUMBERT   Good God—Mona!

MONA   It has been three years since we met. Time cer-tainly flies.

HUMBERT   Let's walk across the campus and have some coffee at The Den.

MONA   I'm afraid I have a class in ten minutes.

HUMBERT   Well, let's go to my office. It's right op-posite.

CUT TO:

Humbert's Office

[194]

HUMBERT   Three long years...

MONA   You don't live on Thayer Street any more?

HUMBERT   Oh no. I've a room in Clemm Hall. And you—how have you been?

MONA   Oh, fine. I left Beardsley School at the same time as—as—anyway, I mean, I never finished Beardsley School.

HUMBERT   I see.

MONA   Your temples are a little gray, which is most becoming.

HUMBERT   You don't ask me an obvious question, Mona.

MONA   Sorry. Have you remarried, sir?

HUMBERT   You haven't changed. Evasive Mona, strange girl.

MONA   I'm not strange. I merely know life rather well. Okay: how's Lolita?

HUMBERT   She's attending a school, a kind of junior college in Europe.

MONA   Oh, so it's true. That's what one of your colleagues told me. What college exactly?

HUMBERT   You would not know it. A small college in Paris.

MONA   Oh.

A pause.

HUMBERT   Old schoolmates seldom write to each other
—isn't that so?

MONA   It depends.

HUMBERT   Naturally. Well, let's chat—let's reminisce,
as Americans say. Why do you look at me like that?

MONA   Mr. Humbert . . . My parents sent me to Europe, too; I, too, went to school in Paris. It's odd that
I never ran into Dolly.

HUMBERT   She never gave you her address, did she?

MONA   Oh, I knew you were still teaching in Beardsley. I could always reach her through you, couldn't I?

HUMBERT   But you didn't.

MONA   Well, no.

HUMBERT   And you completely lost track of her?

MONA   Why don't you give me her address?

HUMBERT   It's hardly worth while: she'll be leaving
next week. As a matter of fact, she may be already in
this country.

MONA   You are still very fond of your stepdaughter,
sir?

HUMBERT   Still? What do you mean—"still"?

MONA   Everybody loves a child, but the child grows up, and something fades, something diminishes.

HUMBERT   Philosophy major.

MONA   But isn't it true? Or would you say that nothing changes?

HUMBERT   Nothing.

MONA   And you'd still be ready to forgive——?

HUMBERT   Forgive? Forgive what?

MONA   We are taking a purely abstract case. Assuming she had done something wrong——

HUMBERT   Mona, will you stop acting the impenetrable vamp?

MONA   Why, everything is crystal clear now. I'm very fond of Dolly, and it's such a comfort to know that you always intend to be kind to her.

HUMBERT   Did she write you? Please, tell me.

MONA   Doesn't she write to *you?*

HUMBERT   She's a poor correspondent—but that's not the point.

MONA   Oh, the point is clear, sir. I'm afraid I must be going now.

HUMBERT   She did write you? You *do* know where
     she is?

MONA   In those faraway schools we were talking about,
     in those schools one can be very unhappy, their lamps
     are dim, but one learns a good deal. I'm sure you
     needn't worry about our Dolly. I've got a class now.

The bell violently rings announcing the beginning of the next
class period.

It should now have been established that Mona has had
a letter from Lolita, apparently asking her to find out if it
is safe for her, Lolita, to write to Humbert.

CUT TO:

University Post Office—The time is 8:55 A.M.
Professor Fowler takes out his letters. Humbert comes up
and tweaks open *his* pigeonhole.

PROFESSOR FOWLER   If your mail is as dull as
     mine, I'm sorry for you, Humbert.

HUMBERT   I never expect anything—that's my advan-
     tage. This is a circular. This is from a Mrs. Richard
     Schiller—some graduate student, I presume. This is a
     fenestrated bill. This is a publisher's list. And this is
     not for me but for Professor Humphries.

FOWLER   Not gay, as the French say.

HUMBERT   Well, I must be rushing to my exam.
     Room 342,
                         (*repeats*)
     342.

[198]

The Door with That Number
He stares at it for a moment.

HUMBERT   How strange.

CUT TO:

A Large Classroom
The questions have been handed out by a monitor, and the examination is under way. Humbert from his lectern morosely observes the bent heads. A crew-cut footballer shoots up an arm, and then buoyantly walks up to the lectern.

FOOTBALLER   It says here, "How did Poe define the Poetic Sentiment"? Do you want us to give a general answer, or actually quote the poem?

HUMBERT   I don't think there is any specific poem implied.

FOOTBALLER   (*utterly at his wit's end but with optimism unshattered*)
I see. Thank you, sir.

He buoyantly walks back to his seat. Humbert, sitting at the lectern, takes his mail out of his pocket and scans it. The monitor turns to the blackboard to write on it "9:10." The footballer, gratefully but mutely, receives from his neighbor a secret note which reads "Poetry is the sentiment of intellectual happiness." The letter that Humbert has opened begins talking to him in a small, matter-of-fact, agonizingly familiar, voice:

LOLITA'S VOICE   Dear Daddy, how's everything? I'm married. I'm Mrs. Richard Schiller. I'm *going to have a baby*. I guess he's going to be a big one. I guess this is a hard letter to write. I'm going nuts because we don't have enough to pay our debts and get out of here. Dick is promised a big job in Alaska, in his specialized corner of the mechanical field. That's all I'm told about it but it's really grand. Please, do send us a check, Dad. We could manage with three or four hundred, or even less. Anything is welcome. I have gone through much sadness and hardship. Your expecting Dolly (Mrs. Richard F. Schiller).

Most of the students having filled a bluebook page in the same number of minutes simultaneously turn it, which makes a brief whistling rustle.

Humbert has risen from his chair, dazed and unstable. He leaves the room followed by all eyes.

CUT TO:

Coalmont—a bleak foggy town

CUT TO:

Hunter Road—a dismal district
all dump and ditch, and wormy vegetable garden. Clapboard shacks line the wasteland. An old man is shoveling mud by the roadside. Humbert speaks to him from his car.

HUMBERT   Would you know if the Schillers live around here?

OLD MAN   (*pointing*) It's the fourth house after the junkyard.

Humbert
driving up to the fourth house. Sounds of hammering and
of two male voices exchanging loud but indistinct comments
come from the back of the shack. Humbert turns off the
motor and for a few seconds sits motionless. A shaggy dog
with a muddy belly comes out and woofs. Humbert fingers
his pistol, transfers it to a handier pocket, gets out of the
car, slamming the door.

DOG   (*perfunctorily*) Woof.

Humbert presses the bell button, keeping one hand in his
pocket.

DOG   Woof, woof.

A rush and a shuffle—the door explodes—and Lolita stands
on the threshold. She wears glasses. She has a new heaped-up
hairdo, new bare ears. She is frankly pregnant. Her pale
arms and neck are bare. But neither the maternity dress nor
the sloppy felt slippers can disguise her Botticellian grace.

LOLITA   (*after a pause, exhaling with all the emphasis
           of wonder and welcome*) We-e-ll!

HUMBERT   (*in a croaking voice*) Husband home?

LOLITA   Come on in.

She lets him pass, crucifying herself against the open door.

LOLITA   (*to the dog*) No, you stay here.

A Small, Shabby, Meagerly Furnished Parlor with the connubial bed disguised as a couch
Lolita, emitting interrogatory "hm's," makes familiar Javanese gestures with her wrists, offering her guest a choice between the couch and the rocker. He chooses the latter.

LOLITA   Dick's mending the back porch with a pal. I'll call him.

She goes out. "Dick!" Dick and a friend come lumbering in. Humbert's hand comes empty out of his trouser pocket. How disappointing!

LOLITA   (*in a resounding violent voice*) Dick, this is my stepfather, Professor Humbert.

DICK   How do you do, Professor.

LOLITA   (*to Humbert*) Dick is very deaf. Speak loud, please. Oh, and this is our kind neighbor, Bill Crest.

BILL   Glad to meet you, Prof.

LOLITA   This calls for a celebration. I'll get some refreshments.

BILL   Let me help you, Dolly.

They go out. Humbert sits in a rocker, Dick on the edge of the couch. He wears overalls, has a shock of dark hair, a nice boyish face. He needs a shave and a hearing aid.

DICK   This is a grand surprise, Professor. Hope you're here to stay. You'll have this couch.

Humbert shakes his head.

DICK   No trouble. We can sleep on a spare mattress in the kitchen.

HUMBERT   I'm on a lecturing tour ...

Lolita and Bill have reentered.

LOLITA   (*very loud*) He's on a lecturing tour. He chanced to visit this town. I wrote him to look us up.

DICK   (*nodding sagely*) I see, I see.

There is a pause. Beer is quaffed. Nobody knows what to say. Lolita greedily crunches potato chips. Bill signals to Dick.

DICK   Well
                (*slapping his knees and rising*)
I guess, you two have a lot to talk about. Come along, Bill. Back to work.
                    (*to Lolita*)
You just holler, sweetheart, when it's time for K.P.

HUMBERT   That's not the fellow I want.

LOLITA   Not *who?*

HUMBERT   You know very well. Where is the swine you eloped with?

LOLITA   (*inclining her head to one side and shaking it in that position*) Look, you are not going to bring that up.

HUMBERT   I certainly am. Three years—during three years I've been trying to find him. Who is he? Where is he?

LOLITA   I should never have written you. Oh, it was a great mistake. Now you are going to spoil everything.

HUMBERT   Could your husband give me that information?

LOLITA   (*blazing and bristling*) Leave out Dick! See? Leave out my poor Dick. He does not know a thing about the whole mess. He thinks I ran away from an upper-class home just to wash dishes in a diner. Why should you make things harder by raking up all that muck?

HUMBERT   Be a sensible girl—if you expect help from me. Come, his name!

LOLITA   (*Half turns away, fumbling for something on a crowded table.*) I thought you had guessed long ago.
                        (*with a mischievous
                        and melancholy smile*)
It's such a sensational name. You would never believe. . . . I can hardly believe it myself—and there's no one I can brag to about it.

HUMBERT   His name, please.

LOLITA   Skip it. It does not matter now. Want a cigarette?

HUMBERT   No. His name.

LOLITA   (*Lights up, shakes her head firmly*) It's too late now to raise hell.

HUMBERT   All right. I'm afraid I must be on my way. Regards to your husband. Nice to have seen you.

LOLITA   Oh, you are so silly to insist. I really should not tell you. On the other hand—do you want to know it that badly? Well, it was——

Softly, confidentially, arching her thin eyebrows and puckering her parched lips, with a note of fastidious, not untender, mockery, she emits in a kind of muted whistle, the name:

LOLITA   —Quilty.

Humbert regards her with stupefaction.

LOLITA   Yes, Clare Quilty, the playwright. Oh, you must have seen his face lots of times in those cigarette ads! And he was staying at that cute hotel at Briceland —remember? And he wrote that play we chose for the Beardsley School show. And he came to rehearsals. And he followed our car in that absurd fashion for miles and miles. Do you know the word "cynic"? Well, that sums him up—a bold laughing cynic. Yes, that's him all over. Clare Quilty. The only man I was ever crazy about.

HUMBERT   There is also Dick.

LOLITA   Oh, Dick is a lamb. We are very happy together. I meant something quite different.

HUMBERT   And *I*? I have never counted, of course?

Lolita considers him for a moment as if trying to grasp the tedious and confusing fact that Humbert had been her lover. That poor romance is dismissed by her like a dull party, a gray picnic, a raindrop of boredom.

He manages to jerk his knee out of the range of a sketchy tap —one of her acquired gestures.

LOLITA   Don't be dense. The past is the past. You've been a good stepdaddy, I guess. Watch your step, Daddy —remember that joke?

HUMBERT   No, that must have been after my time. Where can I find him?

LOLITA   Clare Quilty? Oh, what does it matter? Up in Parkington, I guess. He's got a house there, a regular old castle.
                    (*Gropes and rummages in
                    a pile of magazines on the
                    lower shelf of a console.*)
There was a picture of it somewhere.
                    (*Pulls out a bedraggled
                    issue of* Glance.)
Yes, here it is.

The magazine opens in her slender hands revealing a photograph of Pavor Manor as shown in the first shot of the Prologue. She says with a deep sigh:

LOLITA   This world is just one wild gag after another. If somebody wrote up my life nobody would believe it.

She directs the dart of her cigarette toward the hearth, index rapidly tapping as her mother used to do. Lolita had never smoked under Humbert the Terrible.

HUMBERT   No. I suppose not. Well, let's recapitulate. So it was in Beardsley that you betrayed me.

LOLITA   Betrayed? No. In fact, Cue—everybody called him Cue, you know—Cue was very understanding and sympathetic toward you. You must not tell anybody but many years ago he actually was questioned once by the police about some kid who had complained. So you see you were among friends. Oh, he knew everything about you and me, and it tickled him no end.

She smiles, exhales smoke, shakes her head, darts her cigarette.

LOLITA   You know—that guy saw through everything and everybody. He was not like you or me—he was a genius. He had an Oriental philosophy of life. He believed in Life. Oh, he was—wonderful. Funny—I speak of him in the past as though we were all dead.

HUMBERT   Where exactly did he take you when you gave me the slip?

LOLITA   Yes, that was awfully mean, I must admit that. He took me to a dude ranch near Elphinstone. Duk-Duk Ranch. Silly name.

HUMBERT   Where exactly? What highway?

LOLITA   No highway—a dirt road up a small mountain. Anyway—that ranch does not exist any more. Pity, because it was really something. I mean you can't imagine how utterly lush it was, that ranch, I mean it had everything, but everything, even an indoor waterfall. You know when Cue and I first came the others had us actually go through a coronation ceremony.

HUMBERT   The others? Who were *they?*

LOLITA   Oh, just a bunch of wild kids, and a couple of fat old nudists. And at first everything was just perfect. I was there like a princess, and Cue was to take me to Hollywood, and make a big star of me, and all that. But somehow nothing came of it. And, instead, I was supposed to cooperate with the others in making filthy movies while Cue was gadding about the Lord knows where. Well, when he came back I told him I wanted *him* and not that crowd of perverts, and we had a fight, and he kicked me out, and that's all.

HUMBERT   You could have come back to me.

LOLITA   (*smile, shrug*) Oh, well. . . . I suppose I was afraid you'd kill me. And anyway I was a big girl now, on my own. So—I worked in motels, cleaning up and that sort of job, and in roadside cafés. And then after a year I could not stand it any longer, and thumbed my way back to the place where the ranch should have been. But it just was not there any more, it had burned down completely. So strange.
     (*Smokes meditatively.*)
Well, I drifted back to cheap diners, and one day on the highway Dick picked me up, and we both were lonesome, and so it began.

She closes her eyes leaning back on the cushions of the couch, her belly up, one felted foot on the floor.

"I knew all I wanted to know. I had no intention of torturing my darling. Somewhere, beyond the shack, an after-work radio had begun singing of folly and fate, and there she was with her ruined looks, and her adult rope-veined hands, there she was, my Lolita, hopelessly worn at seventeen—and I looked and looked, and knew that I loved her more than anything I had ever seen, or imagined, or hoped for. . . . She was only the dead-leaf echo of my nymphet— but thank God it was not that echo alone that I worshipped. I loved my Lolita, *this* Lolita, pale and polluted, and big with another's child, but still gray-eyed, still sooty-lashed, still auburn and almond, still Carmencita, still mine. 'Changeons de vie ma Carmen, allons vivre quelque part où nous ne serons jamais séparés' [this is a quotation from Mérimée's novel], no matter, even if those eyes of hers would fade to myopic fish, and her nipples swell and crack—even then I would go mad with tenderness at the mere sight of your dear worn face, at the mere sound of your raucous young voice, my Lolita."

HUMBERT   Lolita, this may be neither here nor there, but I have to say it. Life is very short. From here to that old car there are twenty-five paces. Make them. Now. Right now. Come just as you are. Take that plate of peanuts with you. And we shall live happily ever after.

LOLITA   You mean you'll give us some money only *if?* Only if I go to a motel with you? Is *that* what you mean?

HUMBERT   No, you got it all wrong. I want you to leave your incidental Dick, and this awful hole, and come to live with me, and die with me, and everything with me, eternally. . . .

LOLITA   (*her features working*) You're crazy.

HUMBERT   Think it over, Lolita. I'll wait for any length of time if you want to think. There are no strings attached—except that—well, that a life would be spared. But even if you refuse to come you shall still get your dowry.

LOLITA   No kidding?

HUMBERT   Here. Here's three, four hundred in cash —and here's a check for nine thousand six hundred.

Gingerly, uncertainly, Lolita takes the money, and speaks with agonized emphasis.

LOLITA   You mean you are giving us ten thousand bucks?

He covers his face and breaks into tears. They trickle through his fingers down his chin, his nose is clogged, he can't stop. He gropes for a handkerchief. She touches his wrist. He draws back abruptly.

HUMBERT   I'll die if you touch me. You are sure that you are not coming with me? Is there no hope of your ever coming?

LOLITA   No, honey, no.

His shoulders heave. She provides him with a paper napkin.

LOLITA   No, it's quite out of the question. I'd sooner go back to Quilty. I mean——

HUMBERT   I know. *He* broke your heart. I merely broke your life.

LOLITA   Oh, but everything is so wonderful now. I think it's so utterly grand of you to give us all that dough. It settles everything. We can pay all our debts. We can fly to Alaska tomorrow. Stop crying, please. You should understand. Let me get you some more beer. Oh, don't cry. I'm so sorry I cheated so much—but that's the way things are.

He wipes his face. She smiles at the money.

LOLITA   (*exulting*) May I call Dick?

HUMBERT   No, no. Please don't. I don't want to see him at all. I must leave in a moment.

LOLITA   Oh, don't go yet.

HUMBERT   I love you and this is sheer torture. By the way—about these money matters. There'll be more coming. I must go now.

LOLITA   It has been nice——

HUMBERT   All right, all right.
                   (*evading her hand*)
Yes, good-bye, I have a piece of very important business to take care of. A ragged, raw, horrible piece.

CUT TO:

The Front Porch
A remote sound of voices and hammering comes from the back of the house. The song "Lolita, Lolita, Lolita" is repeated. Lolita and the shaggy dog see Humbert off.

LOLITA   What do you know—the same old car.

HUMBERT   One last word. Are you quite, quite sure that—well, not tomorrow of course, and not after-tomorrow, but some day, any day—you'd not come to live with me? I'll create a brand-new God and thank him with piercing cries, if you give me that small hope.

Lolita smiles, shakes her head in smiling negation.

HUMBERT   It would have made all the difference.

He hurries toward the car.

LOLITA   Good-bye. There's a bad storm coming.

HUMBERT   What?

LOLITA   A storm. Take care of yourself.

Her cry and the sound of the motor attract Bill followed by Dick, as Humbert drives off, with the old shaggy dog loping heavily alongside the car, and soon giving up. We dissolve briefly to Lolita's delirious cry of joy and to Dick's incredulous stare at the gift she brandishes.

CUT TO:

Desolate Road—Storm brewing
Humbert drives off, but a little way down the road, stops and weeps uncontrollably, slumped over the wheel, with the windshield wipers vainly warring against a cloudburst.

A NARRATIONAL VOICE (Dr. Ray's)   Poor Lolita died in childbed a few weeks later, giving birth to a stillborn girl, in Gray Star, a settlement in the remote Northwest. She never learned that Humbert finally tracked down Clare Quilty and killed him. Nor did Humbert know of Lolita's death when shortly before his own dissolution he wrote in prison these last words of his tragic life's story:

HUMBERT'S VOICE   (*clear and firm*) ... While the blood still throbs through my writing hand, you are still as much part of blest matter as I am. I can still talk to you and make you live in the minds of later generations. I'm thinking of aurochs and angels, the secret of durable pigments, prophetic sonnets, the refuge of art. And this is the only immortality you and I may share, my Lolita.

THE END

Revised December 1973
Montreux

VLADIMIR NABOKOV
Summer 1960
Los Angeles

"Nabokov writes prose the only way it should be written,
that is, ecstatically."   —John Updike

ADA, OR ARDOR

A love story troubled by incest, it is also at once a fairy tale, epic,
philosophical treatise on the nature of time, parody of the history of
the novel, and erotic catalog.

Fiction/Literature/0-679-72522-9

BEND SINISTER

Filled with veiled puns and characteristically delightful wordplay,
Bend Sinister is, first and foremost, a haunting and compelling
narrative about a civilized man and his child caught up in the tyranny of a police state.

Fiction/Literature/0-679-72727-2

THE DEFENSE

In this chilling story of obsession and madness, Luzhin, a grand-
master who took up chess as a refuge from the anxiety of his every-
day life, suddenly plummets toward madness during a crucial
championship match.

Fiction/Literature/0-679-72722-1

DESPAIR

Despair is the wickedly inventive and richly derisive story of
Hermann, a man who undertakes the perfect crime: his own murder.

Fiction/Literature/0-679-72343-9

THE ENCHANTER

At once hilarious and chilling, this starkly powerful precursor of
Lolita tells the story of an outwardly respectable man and his fatal
obsession with certain pubescent girls.

Fiction/Literature/0-679-72886-4

THE EYE

As much a farcical detective story as a profoundly refractive tale, *The Eye* is the story of a man who commits suicide, then sets out in the afterlife in search of proof of his own existence.

Fiction/Literature/0-679-72723-X

THE GIFT

Both an ode to Russian literature and one of its major works, this is the story of Fyodor Godunov-Cherdyntsev, an impoverished émigré poet living in Berlin, who dreams of the book he will someday write—a book very much like *The Gift*.

Fiction/Literature/0-679-72725-6

GLORY

Martin Edelweiss is in love with a girl who refuses to marry him. Convinced that his life is about to be wasted and hoping to impress his love, he decides to embark upon a "perilous, daredevil project"—but at a terrible cost.

Fiction/Literature/0-679-72724-8

INVITATION TO A BEHEADING

Cincinnatus C. is condemned to death by beheading for "gnostical turpitude," an imaginary crime that defies definition. Cincinnatus spends his last days in an absurd jail where he is visited by a bizarre collection of people.

Fiction/Literature/0-679-72531-8

KING, QUEEN, KNAVE

Ruddy, self-satisfied, and thoroughly masculine, Dreyer is thoroughly repugnant to his exquisite but cold middle-class wife, Martha, who takes up with his newly arrived nephew, Franz, in what Nabokov called his "gayest novel."

Fiction/Literature/0-679-72340-4

LAUGHTER IN THE DARK

An elegantly sardonic and irresistibly ironic novel of desire, deceit, and deception, *Laughter in the Dark* is also a curious romantic triangle set in the film world of Berlin in the 1930s.

Fiction/Literature/0-679-72450-8

LOLITA

The classic story of the aging Humbert Humbert's obsessive, devouring, and doomed passion for the nymphet Dolores Haze.

Fiction/Literature/0-679-72316-1

LOOK AT THE HARLEQUINS!

As intricate as a house of mirrors, *Look at the Harlequins!* is about Vadim, an author much like Nabokov himself, whose last novel may have crossed the line between fiction and reality.

Fiction/Literature/0-679-72728-0

MARY

In Berlin a vigorous young Russian émigré relives his love affair with Mary, his memories suffused with the freshness of youth, only to discover that the unappealing boarder next door is Mary's husband.

Fiction/Literature/0-679-72620-9

PALE FIRE

In *Pale Fire*, a 999-line poem by the reclusive genius John Shade and an adoring foreword and commentary by his self-styled Boswell, Dr. Charles Kinbote, turn into a darkly comic novel of suspense, literary idolatry, and political intrigue.

Fiction/Literature/0-679-72342-0

PNIN

Pnin is a professor of a language he cannot master, a tireless lover to his treacherous Liza, and the focal point of subtle academic conspiracies he cannot begin to comprehend, yet he stages a faculty party to end all faculty parties forever. .

Fiction/Literature/0-679-72341-2

THE REAL LIFE OF SEBASTIAN KNIGHT

The Real Life of Sebastian Knight is a perversely magical literary detective story—subtle, intricate, leading to a tantalizing climax—about the mysterious life of a famous writer.

Fiction/Literature/0-679-72726-4

SPEAK, MEMORY

Speak, Memory is an elegant and rich remembrance of Nabokov's life and times that also offers insights into his major works.

Autobiography/Literature/0-679-72339-0

THE STORIES OF VLADIMIR NABOKOV

Here the stories of one of the century's greatest prose stylists are collected in a single, comprehensive volume that reminds us that we are in the presence of a magnificent original, a genuine master.

Fiction/Literature/0-679-72997-6

STRONG OPINIONS

In this collection of interviews, articles, and editorials, Nabokov offers his trenchant, witty, and always engaging views on everything from the Russian Revolution to the correct pronunciation of *Lolita*.

Nonfiction/Literature/0-679-72609-8

TRANSPARENT THINGS

A novel of dreams, memory, and the past recaptured—as well as murder, madness, and imprisonment—*Transparent Things* revolves around four trancelike trips to Switzerland.

Fiction/Literature/0-679-72541-5

VINTAGE INTERNATIONAL
Available at your local bookstore, or call toll-free to order:
1-800-793-2665 (credit cards only).

Printed in the United States
by Baker & Taylor Publisher Services